Walking on Air—or on Thin Ice?

"Brittany's just as gorgeous as any of those college girls," Samantha said. "I'm sure she can handle the competition."

"I'm sure she can, too," Kim quickly agreed, but the gleam in her frosty blue eyes said she wouldn't bet on it.

"Don't stay awake nights worrying about my love life, girls," Brittany said lightly. "It's going just fine." She flashed her friends a dazzling smile, but deep inside her, a small, desperate anxiety was growing.

The country club dance was the biggest event of the season. If she was there on Jack Reilly's arm, even Nikki Masters would be eclipsed. He *had* to take her to it. He had to.

Books in the RIVER HEIGHTS® Series

Available from ARCHWAY Paperbacks

RIVER #3 HEIGHTS

GOING TOO FAR

CAROLYN KEENE

AN ARCHWAY PAPERBACK
Published by POCKET BOOKS
New York   London   Toronto   Sydney   Tokyo

AN ARCHWAY PAPERBACK *Original*

An Archway Paperback published by
POCKET BOOKS, a division of Simon & Schuster Inc.
1230 Avenue of the Americas, New York, NY 10020

ISBN: 0-671-67761-6

First Archway Paperback printing January 1990

10 9 8 7 6 5 4 3 2 1

GOING TOO FAR

1

"I just don't know what her problem is, Lacey," Nikki Masters said, switching off the ignition of her car. "Robin's been acting so strange lately!"

"I know," Lacey Dupree agreed. "She's even more wired than usual. And that's saying something."

The two girls stared out the front windshield at the River Heights High parking lot. All around them car doors were being slammed and voices were calling out excited hellos, but Nikki and Lacey were only vaguely aware of the early-morning confusion.

Finally Nikki turned to face her friend.

"This is the third morning Robin has skipped riding to school with us," she said. "She's never had swim practice *every* morning before." Nikki absently ran her hands along the steering wheel. The metallic blue Camaro was a recent birthday gift from her grandfather, but Nikki hadn't gotten her usual pleasure out of driving it that day. She was too worried about her other best friend, Robin Fisher.

Lacey nodded. "Robin's been avoiding us ever since homecoming, and she never *did* tell us what happened the night of the dance —why she never met us."

Nikki sighed. "Every time I try to talk to her, Robin always has some excuse to put me off. She's either with Calvin, or she says she's about to meet him. Or she's at swimming practice or on her way there. One night she said she was washing the dishes, and on Saturday she had to clean her room. If I don't talk to her soon," Nikki finished, "I'll go crazy!"

"Why don't you track her down before homeroom?" Lacey suggested. "She has to be finished with swim practice by now. I'd go with you, but I promised to meet Rick."

"And it's been so long since you two saw each other," Nikki teased. She knew that Lacey and Rick Stratton had been out the night before.

A blush spread slowly over Lacey's delicate, pale complexion. She fingered the end of her long red braid. "I have to work this afternoon. Now is probably the only time I'll get to see Rick all day." Then she grinned at Nikki. "But look who's talking! You've got hours of play rehearsal with Tim this afternoon."

"You're right," Nikki agreed. "I guess I'm just as much in love as you are. Maybe Robin and Cal are having problems, and she doesn't want to tell us about it," she said, frowning.

Lacey shrugged. "Maybe. But they seem as inseparable as ever, if you ask me." She glanced down at her watch. "We'd better get going," she said. "Rick is waiting for me, and you really should try to find Robin."

"Right." Nikki grabbed her backpack and slid out of the driver's seat. After she locked the car, she looked up and spotted Robin heading toward the school.

"There she is, Lacey," Nikki said. "I'm going to try to catch up with her. See you later, okay?"

Not waiting for Lacey to reply, Nikki dashed across the parking lot, weaving between the rows of cars.

"Let me know what happens!" Lacey called after her.

Nikki waved over her shoulder. She didn't want to lose Robin in the crowd of students on the grassy quad. Luckily, Robin Fisher was easy to pick out. Tall, with a terrific figure, short dark hair, and flashing dark eyes, Robin always stood out. And her sense of fashion was pretty wild.

That day Robin's outfit—a Day-Glo green top and lavender-and-orange striped cropped pants—was a bit much, even for Robin. Nikki decided that it was the hot pink high-top sneakers that pushed it over the edge.

"Robin, wait!" Nikki called, hurrying after her.

Robin turned. She was too far away for Nikki to read her expression, but Nikki did see her hesitate. Robin pushed her short dark hair off her forehead in the distracted way that Nikki knew well. She waved back, but continued across the quad toward school.

Nikki's blue eyes clouded over. It wasn't like Robin not to wait for her. Nikki picked up her pace. Whatever was wrong, she knew that Robin needed her and Lacey. The three of them had been best friends a long time.

Slipping one arm through her backpack, Nikki picked her way through the crush of students. The Indian summer weather was perfect for lingering outside, and no one was moving very fast. Her concentration was focused just ahead, and Nikki barely acknowledged the hellos she received. She had only one thought—to catch Robin.

As Nikki pushed through the final knot of kids, she felt Brittany Tate's eyes boring through the back of her head. Nikki tried to appear nonchalant as she kept one eye on Robin's flapping green shirttail. She slowed her pace as Robin stopped to tie a trailing shoelace. There was no need to arouse Brittany's curiosity. Nikki knew that once Brittany's perfect little nose sniffed anything out of the ordinary, she wouldn't stop until she'd hunted down every last detail. Then she'd cheerfully expose the secret to the entire student body through her newspaper column, "Off the Record."

Finally, Nikki caught up to Robin and grabbed her shirttail. "Oh, no, you don't," she said.

Robin turned around, startled. "Uh, hi, Nikki. I'm, uh, late for homeroom——"

Nikki shook her head firmly. "No way, Fisher. We still have ten minutes before the last bell, and I want to know what's up with you. So start talking!"

Brittany Tate's gaze left Nikki Masters, and she turned back to her friends, making sure her thick, dark hair swung gracefully with the movement. She knew the crowd of boys beside the steps was watching her.

Nikki had definitely looked worried, but Brittany decided she couldn't be bothered about that now. Her life was just too busy and interesting to think about Nikki Masters any longer. The poor little thing had probably misplaced her homework.

These days, Brittany had more important things to think about. After all, she was dating a college man.

She turned her attention back to her best friend, blond, beautiful Kim Bishop, who was discussing Brittany's favorite topic—Brittany.

"I knew all along that Jack Reilly was interested in you," Kim was saying. "Even at homecoming you managed to charm him with shaving cream all over your face. Your little scheme that backfired, remember?"

Samantha Daley laughed, shaking her cinnamon brown curls. "Not exactly *my* method of attracting a boy—oh, excuse me, 'man,'" she drawled in her southern accent. Samantha's honeyed tones disguised a mind that could concoct schemes to rival Brittany's.

"Do you know what you're going to wear tonight?" asked Kim.

Brittany shrugged. "I'm not sure. Something sophisticated, though. Jack's taking me to dinner." She paused to let that information sink in. "To dinner" sounded so sophisticated, so much more grown-up than grabbing a pizza or going to a movie. Samantha and Kim looked positively green.

Kim recovered quickly, though, and a sly look crept over her face. "If Jack takes you someplace really elegant, like L'Escargot, I can tell you how to order, Brittany," she offered a little too sweetly. "I was just there for my birthday."

"That's very nice of you, Kim, but I can handle it," Brittany answered smoothly. She hadn't liked the tone in her best friend's voice. She had a feeling Kim was just a little bit jealous. Jack *was* a freshman at Westmoor University, and Kim had never dated a college guy. It was just like her to rub it in that she'd been to plenty of fancy restaurants and Brittany hadn't. Although the Bishops lived in the same neighborhood as the Tates, their home was much grander and they seemed to make a hobby of dining out.

"So, what exactly will you wear?" Samantha asked impatiently. Envy shone through her light brown eyes, too.

Brittany pretended to think, though she'd actually spent days planning her outfit. This would be her first "real" date with Jack. So far they'd only gone out for coffee and shared a few long phone conversations.

"Oh, probably my black leather miniskirt and that new short tuxedo jacket," Brittany replied. She and Kim had both seen the one-of-a-kind jacket the past Saturday at the mall. It was incredibly expensive, but Brittany knew that Kim's mother would buy it for her—even if it cost too much. Brittany had gone back to the mall later that same day and charged the jacket. Her parents hadn't gotten the bill yet, so she knew she had to wear it while she could enjoy it.

"Well, that sounds just perfect," Samantha purred approvingly. "You'll look fabulous."

Kim's ice blue eyes were glinting. Brittany knew her remark about the jacket had hit home, but Kim only smoothed her long blond hair casually. "There's something I've been wondering, though," she said. "About Jack."

Brittany bit her lip. Maybe she shouldn't have mentioned the jacket.

"What is it, Kim?" Samantha asked. Kim always rose to the bait.

"Well, my parents are friends of the Reillys, as you know. We're all members of the country club, and Mrs. Reilly is one of the members of the Committee to Beautify River Heights—along with my mother. So, I wonder if Jack will—well, accept your family. No offense, Brittany, but socially they are kind of out of it." She quickly added, "I mean, your family *could* join the club, if your father wanted to, right? But Jack is such a part of that scene . . ." She left the sentence dangling and shrugged eloquently.

Brittany had to struggle not to throw her math book at Kim's head. Her father simply refused to join the country club. He said he just couldn't be bothered to wear lime green trousers and bat a little white ball around. Her father much preferred working on a broken toaster in the damp basement. Mr. Tate always pointed out that Brittany could go with her friends as a guest whenever she liked. Why couldn't he understand that that wasn't the same thing at all?

Brittany laughed throatily. "Jack seems to be concentrating on me at the moment," she said. "We have better things to talk about than the club."

"I'll bet," Samantha said with a giggle. "College guys must have more important things on their minds."

Brittany gave her a knowing smile, but Samantha's comment made her uneasy. It was an unwelcome reminder that sometimes she didn't know what to say to Jack. She couldn't exactly share River Heights High gossip with a college freshman.

Kim glanced at her expensive tank watch. "I guess we'd better go in," she said.

The three girls turned toward the wide marble stairs that led into the north wing of River Heights High. Kim and Samantha began chatting about Kim's date with Erik Nielson, the cocaptain of the cheerleading squad, the night before. Brittany slung her knapsack over her shoulder nonchalantly, but inside her stomach was in knots as she thought about Kim's comment. Jack probably *was* used to elegance and refinement at home. What would he think of the casual, ordinary Tates?

There was only one solution, Brittany decided grimly. She had to keep Jack away from her family. She'd just have to see that he was so dazzled by her charms that he'd never even ask about her family.

As they started up the stairs, Brittany saw Nikki Masters just off to the side. She was talking rapidly and gesturing in the air, while Robin Fisher stared at the ground. Robin looked especially outlandish that day, Brittany thought, in a green shirt and purple-and-orange pants. Her short brown hair stuck up oddly, as if she'd forgotten to brush it. Nikki's hair, though, looked fantastic, as usual. It shone like spun gold in the sun, and she was wearing a soft rose-colored sweater that Brittany had admired at an expensive boutique in the mall.

Kim leaned close to Brittany. "They ought to issue sunglasses to the whole student body to protect us from the glare," she murmured, nodding toward Robin.

Brittany laughed, and Nikki and Robin glanced up. Robin blushed, but Nikki looked angry.

Brittany felt better as she entered the school. It might just turn out to be a totally fantastic day after all.

"Don't pay any attention to them," Nikki told Robin angrily.

"What were they laughing about?" Robin asked. She looked down at her shirt and pants. A small twinkle lit her dark eyes as she looked back up at Nikki. "We know it couldn't possibly be my clothes."

Nikki laughed. She missed Robin's wise-cracks. She just *had* to get her old friend back again.

"Robin, please tell me what's wrong. You look miserable. Are things okay with you and Cal?"

Robin pressed her lips together. "Nothing's wrong, and I'm not miserable," she finally answered.

"You're giving a real good imitation of a miserable person, then." Nikki hesitated. "Robin," she began in a softer tone, "you have to talk to me. I've been really worried about you ever since homecoming."

Robin looked away. "I'm late."

"Late?" Nikki said. "We have five minutes before homeroom. It's only eight . . ." Her voice trailed away as Robin said nothing. "You mean . . ."

Robin nodded glumly. "My period is late."

Nikki tried to control her shock. "Oh, I didn't know. I mean, I didn't think that you and Cal——"

"We didn't, really," Robin said. "But——"

"But what?" Nikki pressed.

"Oh, come on, Nikki," Robin said. Tears welled up in her dark eyes. "Don't be so—logical!"

Nikki shook her head. "Wait a minute," she said, trying to stay calm. "Let's start over, okay? Why do you think——"

"Everything's a mess," Robin said dramatically, throwing up her hands. "My life is a mess! My relationship with Cal is a mess!" She tugged at her short hair. "Even my hair is a mess."

"Robin," Nikki said, "come to my house this afternoon. No one will be home, and——"

"I have swim practice this afternoon," Robin said, interrupting her.

"Then come after practice," Nikki persisted. "Lacey should be out of work by then, and the three of us can talk. You've got to let Lacey in on this, too. She knows something is wrong."

Robin nodded reluctantly. "All right."

"You'll feel better, I promise," Nikki said.

"Hey, since when have the three of us not worked out a problem?"

"Okay," Robin mumbled. "I'll be over around five-thirty."

"Hang in there, kiddo," Nikki said reassuringly as they started up the stairs. By now everyone else had disappeared into the building. "Help is on the way."

2 〜〜〜

"You both have to swear you'll keep all of this secret," Robin said. She raised her right hand. Nikki and Lacey did the same.

"I swear," the two of them said solemnly.

Robin stretched out her long legs on a multicolored hooked rug in Nikki's bedroom. Nikki and Lacey were sitting cross-legged, facing her. They tried to look hopeful, but Robin could see they were worried. Well, she was worried, too.

Usually, Nikki's room cheered Robin up. It was bright and cozy, with colorful scatter rugs and a quilt handmade in primary colors on the big double bed. The latest magazines were always strewn around, along with Nikki's most recent photographs and lists of things she had to do.

But that day the room was gray in the early twilight. The air had turned chilly outside, and the wind had risen. A bare branch was scraping against a windowpane. Robin shivered. She'd probably caught pneumonia on the way over. Great—just what she needed.

Nikki, seeing Robin shiver, got up and grabbed a peach-colored wool blanket that had been folded on the foot of the bed. "Here, take this. You look cold."

"Thanks." Robin wrapped the blanket around her shoulders. If only Nikki could keep the worry out along with the cold, she thought.

"Let's concentrate on the facts, okay?" Nikki said gently.

Robin shrugged. "It's simple. I'm late," she said. "Very late."

Lacey glanced at Nikki. "I don't think I understand. . . ." Her voice trailed off and her eyes opened wide.

"What don't you understand?" Robin asked.

"Well, what exactly happened between you and Cal," Lacey said. "I had no idea your relationship was so serious."

"We know you care about Cal a lot," Nikki added. "But—"

"But what?" Robin said stonily. Why had she come to Nikki's? She didn't want to answer all these questions. Things with Cal were so wonderful, so scary, and so *private.* When she'd fallen in love with him everything was perfect: those nights at Moon Lake when they'd talked and kissed for hours; every day at school when she'd walked through the halls, hoping for a glimpse of him. She could hardly wait for chemistry lab because they were partners. Lately, though, she couldn't concentrate on anything but Cal.

Her life was going down the tubes. Her grades were slipping. She rarely saw Nikki and Lacey. Even Coach Dixon was on her case in swim practice. How could so many awful things come out of something so wonderful?

"Earth to Robin." Nikki broke into her thoughts. "You were going to tell us why you're freaking out about your late period, remember?"

"Well, we haven't exactly made love," Robin began haltingly.

"Then how?" Lacey started.

"Then why?" Nikki asked at the same time.

Still wrapped in the blanket, Robin rose and began to pace. "I've heard about girls getting pregnant without actually having sex."

"Oh, come on, Robin," Nikki said. "You can't possibly think that——"

"Yes, I can! Of course I can! And I do. Everything in my life is out of control. I'm *scared,* you guys. I feel as if I'm swimming in a race, moving faster and faster, but I can never reach the end of the pool." Robin sighed and plucked at the blanket. "I just wish I'd get my period. I know it sounds crazy, but I know everything would be okay then."

"Have you told your mother about this?" Nikki asked.

Robin shuddered. "Get real. She'd immediately leap to the wrong conclusion."

"Aren't *you?*" Lacey pointed out.

"Don't be so smart, Lacey." Robin glared at her.

"I don't think she would," Nikki said thoughtfully. "If you told her the truth, I'm sure she'd believe you."

"Maybe. *After* she killed me."

Lacey tried another tack. "What about Cal? Have you talked to him about this?"

Robin paced even faster. "I can't tell Cal, either. I'd be too embarrassed. He

thinks I'm worried about the big swim meet.
I am practically living at the pool. Doing
laps is the only thing that makes me feel
better."

"You should talk to Cal," Nikki said.
"Remember when Tim was acting so weird?
I felt awful. *You* were the one who told me to
talk to him."

"Don't remind me." Robin groaned and
sank to the floor again. "I can't believe that
my biggest problem with Cal before this was
that I had to wear flats!"

Nikki and Lacey laughed. Calvin Roth was
an inch shorter than Robin.

"Are you seeing Cal tonight?" Nikki
asked.

Robin shook her head. "We were supposed
to go to the movies, but I cancelled," she
answered. "I have to study. I'm practically
flunking history. What can I say? Everything's wrong in my life—except Cal!"

"I have one more question," Lacey asked.
"Why were you so upset the night of the
homecoming dance? Nikki and I were really
worried. You and Cal never even showed up
till halfway through the dance."

Robin shook her head. "We had a huge fight
that night." She swallowed. "We needed to
be alone for a while to work things out. And
then things got a little carried away." Suddenly she grinned. "I am sorry I missed

Tim's friend Carl making a grand entrance with Brittany Tate."

Nikki laughed. "We couldn't believe it when Brittany turned out to be Carl's 'mystery woman.' I don't think she was very happy about it either." Then Nikki grew serious.

"Robin, I'm sure you'll get your period any day now," she said soothingly.

"I *know* you will," Lacey added, "but you have to relax."

"No problem," Robin said with a groan. She crashed back against the floor and threw the blanket over her face. "I'll just stay here for the rest of the week. Don't worry, Nikki. You can vacuum around me."

Brittany slipped into the tuxedo jacket and turned slowly to inspect her image in the full-length mirror. Perfect. The silky white shirt and short black jacket with satin lapels said sophisticated and elegant. But the form-fitting leather skirt screamed sexy.

She swiveled up her lipstick and applied a light coat to her lips. Just a little makeup, she decided, or she'd look like she was trying too hard.

Brittany glanced at the small enameled clock by her bedside and frowned. She was ready way too early.

So far, though, things were going pretty

smoothly. Her mother had called, saying she was going to work late at her florist shop. Apparently she had to go over the books. Brittany wondered if the shop would have to close. It wouldn't exactly break her heart. Why her mother insisted on running that shop she'd never know. They didn't need the money. And why it had to be in the mall she'd never understand, either. Talk about visible! It was awful. Brittany wanted her mother on committees, like Kim's mother, or working as an artist, like Nikki's mom. But Mrs. Tate loved her little business, and she'd never give it up.

Mr. Tate was late, too. With any luck, he'd come home too tired and distracted to remember that Brittany had a date with a new boy. Hopefully, he'd disappear down to the basement workroom. Then he wouldn't stand around and make jolly conversation with Jack for hours. Time after time, Brittany stood in the hall, waiting while her father became best buddies with her date. Well, it wasn't going to happen with Jack. A college guy wouldn't pal around with a father.

A tap on the door made Brittany start. "Come in," she called.

Her father poked his head around her bedroom door. "Hi, beautiful."

"Hi, Daddy. Hey, you look nice." Brittany's father was wearing a gray suit that was actually presentable. His white shirt was still crisp, and he wore a heavy silk tie in muted grays and violets.

Mr. Tate grinned good-naturedly. "Quite a shock, isn't it?"

Brittany smiled. "Very funny, Dad."

"I had an important meeting with Mr. Masters," Mr. Tate went on. "This is the new suit your mom bought me. Do you like it?"

Brittany had a sudden brainstorm. "I love it. You look fabulous, Dad. So young and handsome. I'd hate to see you change back into your old clothes now." If she flattered her father enough, maybe he'd keep the suit on long enough for Jack to see him in it.

But Mr. Tate was already loosening his tie. "Thanks, Brittany. I can't wait to get out of it, though." He paused. "You look very pretty, I must say. I want to meet this boy, this—"

"Jack Reilly." Sighing, Brittany went back to studying herself in the mirror. Her father was sweet and wonderful, but he was impossible to manipulate. Everything seemed to go right over his head.

"He's coming at six-thirty," Brittany said. "And Mom's going to be late, so she said you and Tamara should cook dinner."

"Oh goody, franks and beans." Mr. Tate waggled his eyebrows up and down and then ambled down the hall.

Franks and beans! Brittany cringed. That summed up everything that was wrong with her family. Her father was thrilled because he got to make his favorite meal. He and Tamara, her thirteen-year-old sister, wouldn't even bother to set the dining room table. They'd eat in the kitchen, laughing uproariously at their own bad jokes. Jack would arrive and the whole noisy house would smell like sauerkraut.

When the doorbell rang at six-twenty, Brittany jumped up. She'd taken off the tuxedo jacket so it wouldn't wrinkle. Now her father or Tamara would get the door. Rats!

Quickly Brittany slipped into the jacket and grabbed her purse, but she could hear her father heading toward the front door downstairs already. Brittany was running down the upstairs hall just as the front door opened. She heard her father's hearty greeting and Jack's reply.

Brittany stopped to catch her breath and smooth her hair. It was too late now; Jack was in her father's clutches. She descended the stairs regally, her hand trailing behind her on the banister.

Her graceful entrance was lost on Jack, however. He was too busy responding to her father's million questions as he followed him into the living room. Brittany saw with horror that not only was her father wearing an old, baggy sweater the color of day-old coffee, but he was also in his stocking feet. She'd never been so mortified in her whole life.

"Hi, Brittany." Jack's brown eyes warmed when she joined them. There was obvious approval in his glance.

"Hi, Jack," she said. "I'm ready to go."

"So you're in Professor Stymist's physics class, then," her father said to Jack. "Good man."

Jack nodded. "I'm enjoying it. I think I might end up going into computers, though."

"It's a great field," Mr. Tate said.

"Dad, we really should be going," Brittany said pointedly.

Mr. Tate stood up. "Oh, sure. Where are you kids headed?"

Kids! Brittany pressed her lips together.

"Well, I thought we'd catch a bite at— Hey, what's this?" Jack stopped and grinned as Tamara raced into the living room in her bright pink socks. She came to a screeching halt when she spotted Jack.

"I didn't realize there were two beauties in the Tate family," Jack said.

That was nice of him, Brittany thought with a sniff. Tamara might share her thick, dark hair and delicately curved mouth, but the resemblance stopped there. Tamara was a grind. Her glasses were about two feet thick, and she had very little interest in boys or clothes. It showed.

"Hello," Tamara said. There was an odd look on her face. "I'm Tamara."

Jack grinned. "Hi, Tamara. I'm Jack."

Tamara took off her glasses and smiled. "You go to Westmoor, right? I want to go there, too, someday."

"You'd better keep your grades up, then," Jack teased, his eyes twinkling.

"Oh, I think she'll have her choice of colleges," Mr. Tate said with a fond glance at Tamara. "She's the studious one."

Brittany wanted to scream. Now not only would Jack think she was a classless hick, but thanks to her father, he'd think she was dumb, too!

Jack reached over and tugged on Tamara's ponytail. "Smart and pretty is a deadly combination," he said. "Watch out, Westmoor."

"I'm really starved," Brittany said, her voice just a tiny bit sharp. When Jack turned, she smiled sweetly at him. "Do you think we could go?"

"Sure," Jack said. "Nice meeting you, Mr. Tate. 'Bye, Tamara."

"Have fun. Good night," Mr. Tate said. He picked up a newspaper from the coffee table.

Tamara seemed tongue-tied. She gazed

wide-eyed at Jack, then followed them to the front door.

"'Bye, Jack," Tamara trilled. "Come again soon."

Brittany bristled, but Jack was shutting the door and didn't notice. Yes, the Tates had done it again. Her father was hopeless, of course. But she couldn't wait to get Tamara alone and straighten the obnoxious little brat out.

"You have a nice family," Jack said.

"Thanks." Wasn't it enough that he'd met them? Did they have to talk about them, too?

"I'm sorry I didn't get to meet your mother," Jack added.

Enough already. "I'm sorry, too," Brittany said sweetly. "She wanted to meet you, but——" She paused. "Mom belongs to so many committees, I lose track of where she is," she finished quickly.

"I know what you mean," Jack said, opening the car door for her. "Our families sound a lot alike."

Brittany was glad the darkness hid her face. Their families *alike!* If only he knew.

Jack walked around the car and slid into the driver's seat. Brittany summoned up every ounce of charm she possessed and put it into her smile. She couldn't waste time worrying about her family now. She had Jack all to herself. It was time to get to work.

3 ⟨~~~⟩

When the phone rang, Robin dove for it. She'd spent the evening staring at one page in her history book, trying not to think about Calvin. Did trying not to think about him count as not thinking about him? She doubted it.

"Robin?"

It was Calvin. "Oh, it's you." The words had popped out before she could stop them.

"Sorry to disappoint you." Calvin's tone was icy.

Terrific, Robin thought. She was off to a great start. "Oh, Cal," she said. "I didn't mean it like that. I thought you might be Nikki. I, uh, need some help studying for my history test."

"Great. Why don't I come over, and—"

Panic ran through Robin. She couldn't see Calvin, not now, not when she was so upset. They'd just get into a fight. "No! I mean, no, I should do it myself. I shouldn't depend on other people to do my homework."

"I know what's wrong with you," Calvin said quietly.

Robin's heart stopped. How could he have guessed? "You do?" she whispered.

"You're suffering from a serious ailment known as rocky road deprivation," Calvin told her.

Robin laughed weakly.

"But I have the solution," Calvin went on. An ice-cream break at Leon's. I'll pick you up in ten minutes, okay?"

Robin's heart beat faster. She wanted to go more than anything, but she was too nervous to have any fun. "Oh, Cal, I'd love it, I really would. But I don't think my hips could stand it."

Calvin paused. "I thought this was Robin Fisher I was talking to. Not Brittany Tate."

"I'm in training, Cal," Robin protested. "You know, for the swim meet. And besides, I really have to study."

"Sure," Calvin said. His voice sounded strange. "I'll see you at school tomorrow, then."

"You bet," Robin said.

There was a long silence. Then Calvin said hesitantly, "Robin, are you okay?"

"I'm fine," she responded quickly. "Just fine. Can't I be nervous sometimes? Do I always have to be Little Miss Perfect?"

Calvin chuckled. "You were never Little Miss Perfect, Robin."

"Oh, thanks," Robin said.

"You know what I mean."

Robin frowned at the receiver. "No, I don't."

"Come on, you know I don't want perfection," Calvin said.

"So you got me instead." Robin's anger rose. "A real lemon. Warranty expired. Think of me as your very own used car. How lucky for you."

"I thought I was lucky," Calvin said stiffly. "Look, I think I'd better get off now. Goodbye, Robin."

"Cal—" Robin began. The word was only half out of her mouth before Calvin hung up. She stood with the phone nestled against her ear, listening to the harsh dial tone.

Great, Robin thought. What more could possibly go wrong?

* * *

The car purred to a stop. Jack turned off the motor and stared at Brittany for a long, delicious moment.

"I had a great time, Jack," Brittany said. It was mostly true. Jack was perfect, there was no doubt about that, but she had a feeling she'd have more fun telling Kim and Samantha about the date than she'd actually had on it.

Jack had taken her to Café Chow, the hip new restaurant where all the college students went. Heads had turned when the two of them walked in, but after they sat down, Brittany realized that everyone else was dressed much more casually.

Maybe she should have asked for Kim's advice on what to order on a sophisticated menu, after all. Brittany had had to ask Jack what radicchio was. She should have kept her mouth shut. It was only Italian lettuce. After that she told Jack that she absolutely adored carpaccio. She'd nearly died when the waiter brought a platter of raw beef to the table!

While she pushed raw beef around her plate and swallowed the bitter lettuce, longing for a cheeseburger or one of Leon's pepperoni pizzas, Jack had talked about the music groups he liked. Brittany had never heard of most of them. When he'd asked what her favorite group was, she'd said the Deadbeats. Jack had smiled and said they'd been his favorites in high school, too. Of course, they weren't very well known two years ago. How embarrassing!

At least Jack's brown eyes seemed appreciative when he looked at her, but Brittany wished she could tell when he was teasing and when he was serious.

Probably since she hadn't been able to talk about new music, Jack had questioned her about her family. Brittany found it easier to talk about them to Jack without their being around. She could evade certain issues, like her mother's business. She did tell the absolute truth about her father's scientific career. He *was* famous in his field. Of course, Brittany did exaggerate by implying that he was practically running Masters Electronics. She'd played up his expertise more than the details of his job, and Jack had been impressed. He was involved in some boring computer project at school, and he'd leaned forward and acted really interested when she talked about some of her father's innovations.

It had definitely been an evening of ups and downs. Now, as they moved across the moon-silvered grass toward her front door, not talking, Jack took her hand. Brittany knew that this was her time. When it came to setting the pace for romance, she was on solid ground.

Well, maybe not completely solid ground. Actually, Brittany felt as if she were floating. Jack Reilly was special. It wasn't just his car or his family's social position—though they didn't hurt, of course. She liked him, the way he held her hand, as if he had a right to. His palm was warm and dry, not sweaty and cold like the ones of the boys she usually dated. She liked Jack's deep brown eyes, and no matter how much his grin unsettled her, she did like how it made her feel when he flashed it.

Jack squeezed her hand as they reached her front porch. Their footsteps slowed, and Brittany's heartbeat quickened, anticipating his kisses as they climbed the steps. It was quiet except for the rustle of the wind in dry autumn leaves. Jack put his hands on her shoulders. She moved a step closer. Once he kissed her, she'd know how he felt about her. She was sure of it!

Jack smiled a slow, drowsy smile. "Well, here we are," he said.

"Here we are," Brittany returned softly, her lips parted. She leaned forward slightly.

Her lips met empty air because Jack suddenly straightened up. "Somebody's still up," he said.

Brittany twisted around, irritated. "It's just my father. That's his study window."

"Oh. He's still awake, then."

"Yes," Brittany said, trying not to sound impatient. Jack was looking over her head. His hands were still on her shoulders, and she moved even closer to him. "But he can't see us," she murmured.

Jack looked down at her at last. There was a light dancing in his brown eyes. "What shouldn't he see, Brittany?" he teased.

Brittany blushed furiously. He was positively infuriating!

"This?" Jack asked. His head dipped down, and he kissed her lightly on the lips. "Or this?" he asked again, his mouth inches from hers. He kissed her again with a bit more pressure.

Brittany's heart thudded much too quickly, and her head whirled. Everything was blotted out but Jack. After a few seconds, he broke away. Brittany felt confused. Didn't he want to keep on kissing her? Usually, she was the one to halt the proceedings.

Gently, Jack reached out and touched her lips with a finger. "I know better places to kiss you than your front porch, Brittany," he murmured. He glanced back up at the study window. "Do you think I could talk to your dad a minute before I leave?"

"What?" This time, Brittany couldn't keep the irritation out of her voice. Jack was all alone with *her,* and he wanted to talk to her *father?*

Jack nodded. "When you were talking about your dad at dinner, I got an idea. It sounds like he could really help me out. I'm designing an entire sound system for this guy in the music department for a project. We're using computers, very sophisticated stuff, but I've run into a few snags. Do you think your dad would mind if we went in and I asked him a few questions?"

Mind? He'd be ecstatic. There was nothing her father liked better than being presented with a problem.

"I guess not," Brittany said reluctantly. She shuddered at the thought of Jack and her father working together in the basement. No, it would never do.

But that was a problem for tomorrow. Now Brittany gave Jack a dazzling smile. "Come on in. I'm sure my dad would be happy to help. It sounds like a wonderful idea."

When Robin's alarm went off the next morning, she sat bolt upright, her heart pounding. She dove for the clock to shut off the harsh, insistent buzz.

She peered at the clock in the gloom. Six-thirty. Way too early, she thought, yawning. But if she didn't improve her times in the pool, Coach Dixon would make her sit out the next meet. *If* she didn't kick Robin off the team. And if she got up now, Robin could get in her training and try to catch Calvin before homeroom to apologize. She'd lain awake for hours worrying about their conversation the night before.

Grabbing the first clothes she found in the closet, Robin dressed hurriedly. If she was down in time, her parents would give her a ride to school. They both went to work at the crack of dawn so that they could be home in time for dinner with the family.

She skidded into the kitchen to find her mother and father sipping coffee and reading the morning paper.

"Morning," Robin said, reaching for the orange juice.

"You're up early again," her father observed. "This must be a trend."

"Are you feeling all right, sweetie?" her mother asked worriedly. "You look a little pale."

"I'm fine," Robin replied. "It's getting up before the sun. I don't know how you guys wake up so early."

"I know how I do it," her mother said, her dark eyes teasing. "I have to take a cold shower every morning. Your father uses all the hot water."

"I do not," her father said in mock outrage. "And *I* make the coffee."

Robin poured herself a bowl of cereal, glad

she'd diverted her parents' attention away from her. "Can you give me a lift to school when you leave, Dad?"

"Sure, honey." Her father checked his watch. "If you can leave in about five minutes. Do you have an early practice again?"

"The earlier I get there, the earlier I get to leave," Robin said. She took another bite of cereal, but she knew she'd never finish the whole bowl. Her stomach was in knots already.

"Do you need to study more before class?" her mother asked. "I know you have that big history test today."

So much for diverting their attention. Her father looked up, suddenly very alert. He was a maniac about grades. "I hope you do well, Robin."

"Thanks, Dad," Robin mumbled. She'd tried to study, she really had, but she hadn't been able to concentrate. It would take a miracle for her to do well on the test.

"I'm sure you'll do just fine," her mother said reassuringly. She patted the top of Robin's head on her way out of the kitchen.

Robin felt like crying. So much for her parents' expectations. Now she had to face Coach Dixon. The last thing Robin expected from this morning was another reassuring pat on the head.

* * *

The smell of chlorine burned Nikki's nostrils as soon as she opened the door to the pool. She spotted Robin immediately by the bright turquoise swimsuit and yellow cap she wore.

Nikki watched as Robin sliced through the water with the clean, powerful crawl that had earned her medals and first-place championships. The air was full of the splashing sounds of swimmers and the yelled instructions of Coach Dixon, who paced back and forth, her compact body tense and her short blond hair slicked straight back.

Nikki sat in the bleachers to wait. She took out a book, but instead of reading, she watched her friend. Back and forth, back and forth. A tidy, perfect racing turn at each end. Back and forth, back and forth.

Finally Robin hauled her dripping body out of the pool. Water streamed down her shapely, muscular legs. She was breathing heavily.

"Not so fast, Fisher." Coach Dixon's voice echoed across the pool. "You may have shown up early, but you're not getting off easy. Ten more laps. And put some muscle into it this time! This isn't a recreational swim!"

Robin turned without a word and slipped into the water again.

By the last lap, Nikki could see how tired

Robin was. Her heart ached for her friend as she hauled herself out of the pool again and looked over at Coach Dixon.

"Hit the showers, Fisher," the coach said in a disgusted voice.

Nikki looked around the bleachers, searching among the piles of white towels strewn there by the swimmers. Then she walked down and picked up the pumpkin-colored towel lying on the front row. She walked to the edge of the pool and handed the towel to Robin without a word.

Robin looked at her in surprise. "How'd you know it was mine?"

Nikki shrugged. "Must have been the quiet, understated color."

Robin grinned. "Yeah, it's pretty dull, all right."

Nikki looked over her shoulder. "Coach Dixon seems out to get you."

"She'll have to get in line." Robin rubbed her hair briskly. "You're looking at a destroyed person, Nikki. I'm losing my boyfriend, my good grades, and now my crawl and backstroke. What's left?"

Distressed, Nikki gazed at her friend's unhappy face. How could she cheer Robin up? Then she snapped her fingers. "I'll tell you what's left, Rob. Shopping!"

4 ~~

That day after school the Southside Mall was even more jammed than usual.

"I knew this was a mistake," Robin said listlessly as she and Nikki came out of Glad Rags. "There isn't one decent piece of clothing left in the whole mall."

Nikki's face fell, and Robin regretted her words immediately. Nikki was only trying to be nice. "I'm sorry, Nik. I'm awful. All I do is complain. I'm such a jerk."

"No, it's been fun," Nikki said soothingly.

"Come on, don't start lying to me, Masters," Robin said.

"Okay, you've been a jerk," Nikki admitted, laughing. "But it's okay," she added, taking Robin's arm. She pulled her back into the meandering flow of mall traffic. "Let's go see Lacey."

Robin glanced over at Platters, the record store where Lacey worked. The store was jammed. Through the window she could see Lacey furiously totaling up purchases, her fingers flying over the cash register buttons.

"I think Lacey's pretty busy right now," Robin said. "Maybe we shouldn't bother her."

"She'll meet us tonight at my house, anyway," Nikki told her. "She's picking up a video for us after work. You are still coming over, aren't you?"

Robin nodded. "Sure, but I'm going to grab some ice cream with Cal first. I promised him this morning when we made up."

Nikki groaned. "Now we'll never see you."

"No, I'm definitely coming," Robin promised. "I wouldn't miss it. The three of us haven't had an evening together in so long." She grinned. "Who knows what Lacey will pick out for us to watch this time?"

Nikki laughed. Whenever Lacey chose a video, she made the craziest choices. The three of them had sat through quite a few clunkers.

"Do you want to try Josie's now?" Nikki asked, referring to a shop with casual clothing.

Robin hesitated. "I don't think so, Nikki. I'm not really in the mood to shop. I should probably just go home and get some studying in before dinner."

"Okay," Nikki agreed. "Would you mind stopping in the drugstore with me first? My mom asked me to pick up a few things."

Robin nodded and followed Nikki inside. She was browsing through the shampoos when she suddenly felt Nikki tug at her elbow.

"What is it?" Robin asked.

"I have the solution to your problem," Nikki announced in a low voice. "I don't know why we didn't think of it before."

"What?" Robin demanded.

Nikki held up a cardboard package. "It's one of those kits," she explained. "You know, so you can test yourself at home to see if you're pregnant. This might be the solution to your problem."

Brittany was glowing. She was at the mall with Jack Reilly, and everyone from school knew it. As she and Jack strolled past the shops, she saw heads come together and then heard the buzz of whispered conversation. Brittany practically floated through the mall.

Jack had been waiting outside River Heights High when she left the building. He'd been the one to suggest the mall. Brittany had hoped plenty of kids would be around to see them, but this was even better than she'd imagined.

The only problem could be if they had to pass Blooms and her mom saw them. Her mother's shop was hard to miss. Buckets of flowers and, at this time of year, tall branches with silver green leaves from various exotic shrubs would be on display. Brittany could never remember the names of any of them, no matter how many times her mother tried to drum them into her head. She hoped Jack wasn't fond of flowers.

As they passed the fountain, Brittany glimpsed Kim and Samantha sitting on a bench, spooning up frozen yogurt. She pretended not to see them and slipped her hand into Jack's.

"Your dad," Jack was saying. "What a guy. In two minutes he figured out the solution to a major problem. He's just amazing. We're going to work in your basement tonight."

"That's great," Brittany said weakly. "I'm glad he could help you."

Jack swung her hand as they walked. "He's got a terrific daughter, too."

"Oh?" Brittany batted her lashes ever so slightly.

"Yeah, that Tamara is quite a charmer," Jack said mischievously.

Brittany laughed and punched him teasingly on the arm, but she felt her heart fall. She knew Jack was teasing, of course, but she wished he would be serious sometimes.

He led them right at the next corner. Oh, no! Brittany had been so preoccupied that she didn't realize how close they were getting to Blooms. The shop was just ahead!

Brittany thought furiously. "Oh, Jack, I'm dying to show you this store," she blurted out. She tugged on his hand and led him over to a store opposite Blooms. Luckily there was something to look at! The shop had high-tech lamps and furniture, all the latest in modern design.

"I like this store, too," Jack said. "They have some cool things."

Brittany was examining a streamlined couch in gray tweed fabric when she realized, to her horror, that they were clearly reflected in the store window. Her mom could see them.

"Maybe we should—" she started.

"Hey!" Jack said, spinning around. "Look at all those flowers. They're incredible." He looked at Brittany and grinned. "Come on, I'm going to buy you a present. Just to show you I can be a nice guy."

Under normal circumstances, Brittany might have swooned. It was about time Jack showed his romantic side. But right then she was frantic. What could she do?

"Oh, Jack, that's so sweet," she said quickly. "But you know what I'd *really* like? More than flowers, even?" She paused, racking her brain. "Chocolate!"

Jack looked amused. "Chocolate?"

Brittany nodded vigorously. "It's my ultimate weakness. I just can't resist it. Besides," she said, improvising, "I'm, uh, allergic to flowers."

"Too bad," Jack said. "So you're a pushover for sweets, huh?"

"Mmmm. You can't imagine." She looked up at him through her eyelashes. "I just melt."

"Well," Jack said softly, brushing a strand of dark hair away from her cheek, "I think I'll tempt you then. What would you like?"

Brittany thought fast. She never ate sweets, but getting Jack away from Blooms was worth an extra ounce or two. "Oh, the drugstore up on the next level has some wonderful imported Swiss chocolate bars," she told him. "I just love them."

"You're on," Jack said, tucking her arm into his. "We're off to the drugstore."

Robin stared at the package in Nikki's hand and shook her head slowly. "No way."

Nikki frowned. "Robin, *I* know you're not pregnant, but *you* need to know it."

"I can't, Nikki." Robin looked down at the floor.

Nikki looked exasperated. "Why not? It's easy. You can do it at my house—no one will ever know."

"Shhhh." Robin cautioned her to be quiet as a woman turned the corner, pushing a toddler in a stroller. Grabbing Nikki's sleeve, Robin led her farther down the aisle. "Look, Nikki, you should know something. I'm a low-down coward."

"That's ridiculous," Nikki began.

"If I don't know for sure, I can tell myself that I'm not," Robin hissed.

"But you're telling yourself that you *are!*" Nikki pointed out. "You're not making any sense, Robin."

"I know," Robin said mournfully. She nodded toward the box. "Now put that thing back."

"Here, just read the label." Before Robin could protest, Nikki thrust the box into her hands. "There are other ones," Nikki explained, "but I saw this one advertised on

TV. Look, there's even a toll-free number you can call if you have any questions. Read the directions, Robin. It sounds so fast and easy."

Robin gazed uneasily around the store. Her earrings, small plastic solar systems with orbiting planets, banged against her cheeks. "Oh, Nikki, I can't buy this. I'm too scared. Someone's going to *see* us, I know it."

"No one will see us," Nikki assured her. "Come on, let's go to the register and buy it."

Robin hesitated. "I don't know. Let me think. I should buy a couple of other things first." Robin started to pull things down from the shelves. "I mean, I definitely need shampoo. Oh, and I wanted to try this mousse. Look—this conditioner is supposed to be great. My hair is a limp wreck from all the swimming I've been doing. What I really need is gel." Robin was filling her arms while she talked.

"For heaven's sake," Nikki said. "You're going to clean out the store! You don't have to buy the kit, Robin. Forget I brought it up."

"Okay, okay," Robin muttered. "Let's just go home. I'd need to hear the verdict from some authority figure in a white coat, anyway." Her arms filled with tubes and bottles, Robin tried to pluck the kit out of the pile. "Will you put it back for me?"

As Nikki nodded, the toddler they'd seen earlier came barreling around the corner, this time gleefully pushing his own stroller. Missing the girls by inches, he rammed the stroller into a free-standing cardboard display of film. It instantly began to topple. Instinctively Robin reached out to steady it. Down clattered her tubes and bottles as the display fell and packages of film tumbled into the confusion of goods. The pregnancy test kit flew through the air and landed by itself in the middle of the aisle.

"Oh, no," Robin groaned. She fell to her knees and started crawling toward the pregnancy kit, picking up bottles of conditioner and shampoo on her way.

The toddler's mother turned the corner and shrieked. Then, seeing her child was safe, she ran toward Nikki and Robin. "Tommy can be a bit too lively," she said.

"He's adorable," Robin said through clenched teeth. "Look, if you could just move to the left—"

But the woman moved to the right to pick up a shampoo bottle and got in her way again. Robin groaned. Why didn't Nikki run and pick up the box? But Nikki hadn't noticed Robin's predicament; she was trying to right the cardboard film display.

Forcing a smile, Robin juggled the tubes and bottles as the woman handed them to her. Her cheeks felt hot, and she knew from experience that her face was probably as purple as a Bermuda onion.

The woman stood up then, just as Nikki was replacing the last box of film. Tommy the toddler chuckled and took off with the stroller again. Robin finally made her way down the aisle to pick up the telltale kit. But as she reached for the box, she felt sure that someone was watching her. Robin looked up to find herself staring right into the shrewd dark eyes of Brittany Tate.

"Is this the kind you like?" Jack asked.

"Sure," Brittany replied absently. Her eyes were fixed on Robin Fisher. She was kneeling on the floor with a pregnancy test kit in her hand. She looked positively horrified as she shoved the box behind her and sent it sailing across the slippery floor toward Nikki Masters. Who did those two think they were fooling?

Nikki waved and smiled. Even Robin tried to grin as she rose to her feet. "Hi, Brittany," they called. Then they turned and scurried back down the aisle, dropping tubes of mousse and bottles of shampoo into their slots on the shelves.

"Hey, wasn't that Nikki Masters?" Jack asked. "She was on the homecoming committee with us."

"Yes," Brittany answered, distracted. She was trying to think. Who would have guessed that Nikki Masters or one of Nikki's friends would get into *that* kind of trouble?

There could be no other explanation. Why else would they be buying that test? As Jack went off to pay for the candy, Brittany tried to figure out which girl it could be.

Maybe Nikki and Tim Cooper had gotten a little too close, but Robin's romance with Calvin Roth was pretty hot and heavy, too. Then there was Lacey Dupree. She saw quite a bit of Rick Stratton, didn't she? Spacey Lacey, Brittany had dubbed her, but she'd always thought that there was more behind that pale, romantic-looking girl than met the eye.

So it was either the Moose, the Mouse, or the Barbie Doll. Oh, Brittany thought, the possibilities were delicious. Just delicious.

"Brittany, here." Jack handed her the chocolate bar. She smiled and dutifully tore open the wrapper. Did she really have to eat it? It was bad for her figure and worse for her complexion.

Jack bit into his bar enthusiastically. "This is great," he said, chewing. "You were right."

Brittany nibbled delicately at hers. "Mmmm," she said. "It's fabulous."

Now that she had this tantalizing bit of

information about Nikki or her friends, what should she do with it? She could keep it to herself, of course. That would be the fair thing to do, she mused as they left the store and wandered back out into the mall. There was no sign of Robin and Nikki. They'd beaten a hasty retreat, of course.

"Here, taste mine," Jack said, startling Brittany from her thoughts. "It has macadamia nuts in it."

Brittany leaned over and took a bite of Jack's candy. Here she was, putting on pounds and pimples because she had to keep her mother's business a secret. She'd have to skip dinner to make up for all the calories she was consuming. It wasn't fair. Her life wasn't fair. So why should Nikki Masters's life be fair?

Over Jack's shoulder, Brittany spied Kim and Samantha coming out of Platters, looking sulky and bored to death. Perfect! "Oh, Jack," Brittany said, laying a hand on his arm, "I see my friend Kim over there by the fountain. Would you mind if I went over and spoke to her for a minute?"

Jack grinned his okay. "Don't be long," he told her.

"Oh, this won't take very long at all," Brittany replied sweetly.

5 ～～～

Robin and Nikki waited until they were on the lower level of the mall to discuss the catastrophe.

Robin clutched Nikki's arm. "You're *sure* she didn't see it?"

"She couldn't have," Nikki said. "I mean, she was all the way over by the candy."

Robin groaned. "I don't know. Old eagle-eye Tate doesn't miss a trick."

"I'm sure she missed this one," Nikki declared confidently.

"Are you *positive?*" Robin persisted.

"Robin, I really don't think she saw anything."

"You don't *think!* Then she could have!" Robin wailed. "Nikki, what if she puts it in her column? You know, 'Off the Record.'"

Nikki shook her head. "No way. Even Brittany isn't that low, Robin."

"You're always too easy on her," Robin said. "Look what she's done to you, Nikki! She tried to take Tim away and then she tried to humiliate you at homecoming. *Nothing* is too low for Brittany Tate." Robin glanced around uneasily. "I feel so conspicuous. Like there are a thousand eyes on us in this mall, and everybody *knows.*"

"Don't be silly," Nikki said. "Brittany wouldn't even have had time to tell anyone yet. I mean," she added quickly, *"if* she saw. Which she didn't. Now, let's go home."

"If Brittany told some gossip hound like Samantha Daley or Jeremy Pratt, it could be on the evening news," Robin said grumpily as they moved toward the exit. "I'm dead meat. Let's face it."

"That's enough, Robin," Nikki said sternly. "Nobody knows anything. You're really getting paranoid. Your secret is absolutely safe!"

"No!" Samantha gushed. "Which one?" Brittany shrugged and moved a little closer to Samantha and Kim. "It could be any one of them, couldn't it?"

"This is some piece of news," Kim said breathily. "I just can't believe it."

"It couldn't be Nikki," Samantha said decidedly.

Brittany gave her a scornful look, but she remained silent. Let her friends draw their own conclusions. Besides, she was beginning to feel a little bit guilty about spilling the beans.

"Look, there's Cheryl Worth over there," Kim said. "I wonder if she's heard."

"Of course she hasn't," Brittany said uneasily. "I only told you two. It's not the kind of news you spread around."

"That's true," Samantha said, her eyes roaming over the mall.

"Well, I have to get back to Jack," Brittany said hesitantly.

"Yes, go ahead, Brittany," Kim said cheerfully with a wave of her hand. "Jack looks impatient, and we were just about to give Cheryl a ride home."

"Well, okay. 'Bye." Brittany watched as her friends crossed the mall, Kim with her casual, assured stride, Samantha scurrying behind her. Brittany felt a slight pang of remorse. She'd die if a rumor like that got around about *her*.

* * *

When Brittany and Jack drove home from the mall, Brittany decided that now was the time to try out her plan.

Jack walked her to her front door. "I'll take off now," he said. "I have to get in some studying. But I'll be back tonight to see your dad, so I'll get to see you then."

Brittany let a shadow cross her face. "Right," she said hesitantly.

Jack cocked his head at her. "Hey, are you tired of me already?" he asked, joking.

"Oh, no," Brittany assured him. "It's nothing like that." She looked down.

Jack raised her chin with his finger. "What is it, Brittany? Tell me."

She sighed heavily. "Come in the backyard for a minute, Jack. I have to talk to you in private."

"Sure."

Brittany could tell that Jack was puzzled as they rounded the corner of the house. They walked down the lawn to the garden.

"This is my favorite spot," Brittany confessed shyly.

"I thought you were allergic to flowers," Jack said, frowning.

"That's why I can only come here in the fall," Brittany told him without missing a beat.

Jack seemed to think that made sense. "So

what did you want to talk to me about, Brittany?"

"Well, it's my father, actually," Brittany began slowly. "You see, he had a checkup recently, and—"

"He's all right, I hope," Jack said quickly.

Good. He looked concerned. Brittany nodded. "Oh, yes, he'll be fine, if—"

"If?" Jack prompted.

Brittany twisted her hands. She'd better make this good; she didn't want to overdo it. "Well, Jack, my father works very hard. He's a genius at scientific research, and he's absolutely *driven*. Even when he gets home from work, he keeps on going. This project, that project—" Brittany shrugged. "He just never stops. We're all so worried about him. The doctor says he's got to slow down. When he gets home, he should read the newspaper, watch TV, spend time with the family—you know. But he disappears into the basement all night, working." Brittany dashed away a nonexistent tear. "I just don't know what to do, Jack."

Jack's brown eyes warmed with concern. "I'm so sorry, Brittany. I know how you feel. My father works like crazy, too. I wish there was something I could do." Jack put his arm around her and she sniffed.

"Thanks for understanding," Brittany murmured, her cheek against Jack's sweater.

She waited for Jack to put the pieces together. "It's just that my dad's so stubborn," she added. "If only he wouldn't work at night, at least." There—she'd done all she could. Would he get it?

Jack frowned. "Maybe I can help you, after all."

"Oh?" she asked, feigning a puzzled look.

"I'll tell your dad I don't need his help on my project. It will be one less thing for him to worry about, anyway."

Brittany stepped away. "Oh, no. I didn't mean— I couldn't let you do that, Jack. I know how important this project is to you."

"Don't be silly," he said, waving a hand. "I should figure it out myself, anyway."

"No," Brittany said, shaking her head. "Absolutely not. I won't let you."

"You have to," Jack said firmly. "I insist. Do you think I'm a selfish brute?" He grinned. "Don't answer that. I am not going to add to your father's work load. Besides," he said, gazing at Brittany with a tender look that made her heart flip over, "I've never seen you upset like this. The decision's final."

"Oh, Jack. I *do* feel better. Thank you. You're so sweet." Brittany stepped toward him and brushed her lips against his cheek. Jack stepped closer, but Brittany reluctantly edged away and began to walk back toward the house. You have to flee if you want to be pursued, she reminded herself.

"This is such a nice house," Jack said as they walked up the lawn. "That sunporch is great."

"Yes, we like it," Brittany said. "We're thinking of selling the place, though." *She* was trying to talk her father into selling, that was.

Jack raised his eyebrows. "You wouldn't move away?"

"Oh, we won't leave River Heights," Brittany assured him. She paused by the big oak tree. "It's just that this house is a little small for us, and in the wrong location. My father would like to move to a different neighborhood. Nearer to the country club, of course," she added offhandedly. If Jack wanted to think the Tates were members, he could. The area around the country club was where Brittany wanted to live. Even if she had to be a neighbor of Nikki Masters's.

"Sounds good to me. That's where I live." Jack squeezed her hand.

"And we'd be nearer to the Masterses and the Drews," Brittany added nonchalantly.

"Oh, is your dad a friend of Carson Drew's?"

"Mmmmm," Brittany answered noncommittally. "And, of course, I know Nancy."

She didn't mention that they weren't friendly at all.

"Nancy's terrific," Jack said. "I see her at the club a lot. She plays a mean game of tennis. Beats me every time. But I like her anyway."

Brittany suddenly wondered whether Jack was thinking that he never saw *her* at the club. Should she say that they were new members? Or that she didn't go much?

Just then she caught sight of Tamara's sneaker sticking out from behind an oak tree. Had her snooping little sister heard their conversation?

"Tamara!" she called. "What are you doing over there?"

"Nothing," Tamara said, stepping out from behind the tree. Her eyes were trained on Jack. "Hi, Jack."

"Hi, Tamara," Jack replied easily. "How're you doing?"

"Fine," Tamara said. "How are *you*?"

"Just fine," Jack said. "What's up with you today?"

Brittany rolled her eyes. This could go on all afternoon. "Don't you have *homework* to do?" she asked Tamara. She jerked her head toward the house.

Tamara ignored her and turned back to Jack. "I'm not up to anything much. I just like being outside. Autumn's my favorite season. What's yours, Jack?"

"I like summer," Jack answered amiably.

Brittany tried to conceal her annoyance at this fascinating exchange. She pressed Jack's arm. "Come on, Jack, let's go inside."

"All right," Jack said. "I'll have a word with your father, and then I'd better get going."

"Are you coming back later tonight, Jack?" Tamara asked.

"No, I'm afraid not," Jack replied. "I'm not going to be working with your dad after all."

Tamara frowned. "Why not? He was really looking forward to it. He's got all these notes—"

"Tamara, Jack's in a hurry." Brittany started to walk quickly toward the house, and Jack had to follow. She'd have to do something about that brat, and soon.

By the time Calvin dropped Robin off at Nikki's house, Robin felt limp with exhaustion. She'd tried hard to make the date fun and upbeat, but she had a feeling Calvin knew she was upset anyway. Especially after she dropped her triple cone of rocky road on his white shirt.

She said a quick hello to Nikki's parents and ran up the stairs to Nikki's bedroom. As soon as she was through the doorway, she burst into tears.

Nikki jumped up from her desk and ran over to her. "Robin, what is it?"

"My date with Cal was a fiasco," Robin wailed. "Things are going from worse to worst." She dropped onto the bed.

"Oh, Robin." Nikki went over to the night table and came back with a box of tissues. She tossed them in Robin's lap, then waited while Robin blew her nose vigorously and wiped her tears.

When Robin felt calmer, she glanced at Nikki. "Uh-oh," she said. "I think I'm about to get a lecture."

"Not a lecture," Nikki replied. Her voice was gentle. "But, Robin, why don't you tell Cal what's wrong? Don't you think he should know?"

Robin shrugged. "Know what? There's nothing to know yet." She stood up and began to pace the room. "I love Cal, I'm crazy about him, and I don't want him to be going through what I'm going through. Does that make any sense?"

Nikki nodded. "That's very considerate. But, Robin, suppose nothing is wrong, which I'm sure is true. You could drive Cal away."

Robin flopped down on the bed again. "As soon as I get my period, I'll be back to normal."

"I know that," Nikki said patiently, "but imagine how Cal would feel. One day you jump down his throat, and the next you're sweet as pie. Shouldn't he know *why* you've been acting so weird? He has no idea what's going on. By the time you're feeling better, he might be afraid to trust you again," she added gently.

Robin frowned. "Is this supposed to make me feel better, Nikki?"

"Okay, okay. I'm sorry," Nikki said. "Just think about it, that's all."

Robin gnawed furiously on a fingernail. "I appreciate the advice, Nikki, I really do. But I just can't think straight right now."

Suddenly the door flew open and Lacey burst into the room, panting. "I've got news," she gasped, flinging herself onto the bed next to Robin.

"Good or bad?" Nikki asked.

Lacey struggled to catch her breath. "Not good," she managed to say.

Robin shrugged. "No problem. Give it to us straight. I might be pregnant. What could be worse?"

Lacey hesitated.

"Lacey?" Robin prodded.

"Something worse? How about everyone at school wondering if you're pregnant, too?"

Robin's mouth dropped open. "Tell me you're kidding," she whispered.

Slowly Lacey shook her head. "It's not just you, though," she said. "Me and Nikki, too. We're all under suspicion. How did this happen?"

Nikki and Robin exchanged glances.

"Brittany Tate," they said together.

"I don't know who started the rumor," Lacey said, "but it's all over the mall. Everybody's talking about us. We're the hot news at River Heights High!"

Robin slid off the bed. "It's over! I'm finished!" she moaned. She looked at Nikki hopefully. "Do you think my parents would move to Chicago tomorrow if I asked nicely enough?"

"I don't think so," Nikki said sorrowfully.

"Then *I'll* move," Robin said. "To Siberia or Karachi or Dar es Salaam!"

"You may be flunking history, but you're great at geography," Lacey said.

Robin glared at her. "You don't understand, Lacey. I can't go back to school tomorrow!"

Lacey raised her eyebrows. "Aren't you forgetting something, Fisher? We're all in this together."

Robin raised herself on her elbows. How could she have forgotten that this was a disaster for Nikki and Lacey, too?

"It's true, Robin," Nikki said. "Lacey and I are in the same boat. Nobody knows which one of us the rumor is about." Dawning horror widened her eyes. "Tim!" she exclaimed. "What will *he* think?"

Lacey paled. "Rick!"

Robin sat bolt upright. "Cal!" she cried.

The three girls stared at one another.

"We'll just have to tell them what happened," Nikki decided. "Except—" She paused, a sly look stealing over her face.

"Except what?" Lacey demanded.

Nikki grinned. "We'll ask them not to set

anybody straight. Let everyone wonder. We'll act so happy and casual that nobody will be able to guess!"

Robin gulped. "Happy?"

"Nikki, you're a genius," Lacey said. "That'll take the heat off Robin!"

Robin shook her head. "I can't let you guys do it. You can't ruin your reputations for me."

"Don't argue," Nikki said. "It's the only way. Besides, those nasty gossips deserve a little confusion."

"Don't you see, Robin?" Lacey said. "It's the perfect plan. Because pretty soon, they'll realize that they were wrong anyway. And Brittany Tate will just look bad!"

"But what if we can't pull it off?" Robin asked nervously.

Lacey's blue eyes twinkled. "There's always Dar es Salaam," she said.

The next morning Robin concentrated on coordinating her clothes. Nikki had pointed out that her outfits had been a little, well, odd lately. That day, at least, it was important to match. She didn't want to attract any more stares than she was going to receive already.

She pulled on a pair of slim black pants, a white T-shirt, and a man's jacket from the fifties in iridescent purple. Defiantly, she rummaged through her jewelry box for her wildest earrings. It wasn't until she slid into the back seat of Nikki's car that she realized she'd forgotten one of them.

"How do I look?" she asked Nikki and Lacey.

Lacey looked pointedly at the purple jacket. "Positively preppie," she said.

"You look terrific," Nikki told her. She swung the car into traffic and headed toward school.

Robin resisted an impulse to plead for Nikki to head for the lake instead. *Anywhere* but River Heights High. Despite their agreement the night before, despite her friends' support, she was terrified.

"You know, it might not be bad," Lacey said cheerfully. "Maybe people will be nice."

Robin cranked down the window to let the wind blow her hair dry. "Thanks for trying, Lacey," she said gloomily. "But we all know this news is too hot to resist."

Nobody spoke for the rest of the short drive. Nikki pulled the Camaro into the parking lot, and the girls silently gathered up their books.

Every head on the quad must have turned as the three of them started across the parking lot. Robin froze in her tracks. "I can't," she said desperately. "Look at them. They're going to eat us alive."

Lacey put a strong hand on her sleeve.

"Don't be a jerk," she said. Her soft voice had an edge of steel. "We can do it. Let's keep them guessing, okay?"

Robin felt her eyes fill. "You guys are the best friends in the world," she whispered.

"If you cry, I'll kill you," Lacey answered serenely. "Now, let's go."

The three of them moved together, shoulder to shoulder, across the quad. Robin could see Brittany's mouth moving a million miles a minute as she entertained a small clot of students.

"Let's start talking," Lacey said, smiling for the benefit of anyone watching. "It doesn't matter about what. Let them think we don't have a care in the world."

Lacey began a conversation, and Nikki determinedly joined. Whenever there was a lull, Lacey's quiet voice sailed in and filled it. Every once in a while Robin even laughed. The three of them talked and talked as though it were a normal day. Almost.

But when Robin found herself alone at her locker, surrounded by students who were probably watching her every move, she felt her nerve fail.

"You can do it, Fisher," she muttered as she slammed her locker door closed.

"Are you okay, Robin?" Samantha Daley

appeared out of nowhere and hovered next to her, peering at Robin with fake concern.

"I'm fine," Robin snapped. Then she remembered Lacey's steel calm. Robin leaned closer and peered at Samantha. "How are *you,* though? You look awfully pale."

Samantha's cinnamon brown eyes narrowed, and she quickly went back to her own locker. Robin left her applying blush and scrutinizing her face from all angles in her compact mirror. Score one for us, Robin thought as she headed for her homeroom. But she didn't feel cheered. It wasn't even nine o'clock yet. She had a long way to go.

Nikki felt as though she were trapped in a nightmare. As she moved through the halls, some people looked away or only mumbled their hellos. How could this be happening to her again?

She'd put on a brave front for Robin and Lacey, but she was terrified. This situation had brought back painful memories from the beginning of the school year. Nancy Drew had cleared Nikki of the charge of murdering her old boyfriend, but even Nancy couldn't dispel the dark clouds of gossip that had followed Nikki. Nikki would never forget the stares and whispers. It was funny that Brittany Tate had been the one to force everyone to stop talking about Nikki on the first day of school.

But now, Brittany had started an ugly rumor. Nikki decided she'd never figure that girl out—she, Robin, and Lacey were in for one very tough day.

As she walked through the hall to her honors English class, Nikki thought about Tim. He'd been late to school, so she hadn't seen him in homeroom. She sat next to him in English, though. Would he have heard the rumors already? How could she explain the situation to him? Tim had always been so understanding, but this might be too much for even him to handle.

Then she saw him, brushing his way past students as he hurried toward her. His handsome face looked tense, and his gray eyes were as steely and bleak as a winter sky. Was he angry at her? Nikki wondered, her heart pounding against her chest.

Tim stopped and then swung into step beside her. "I heard," he said tersely. "I can't believe what people are saying! I want to get on the P.A. and tell everyone it's not true. How did this get started, Nikki?" He linked his arm with hers, and Nikki felt relief and love sweep over her. The strong, reassuring pressure of Tim's arm against hers brought all her strength back.

"I'll tell you everything after class," she said. "But there's nothing we can do."

"For this to happen to you . . ." Tim shook his head. "I'm going to tell everyone I see that I know for sure it's not true about you," Tim said.

"Don't do that," Nikki said quickly. "I mean, I don't want you to say anything."

Tim gazed at her, dumbfounded. "Why not? They think—"

"I know what they think," Nikki said steadily. "Let them."

"But why?" Tim asked.

"Let's just say it'll make things easier for a friend," Nikki answered. Her eyes pleaded for him to understand.

Tim looked serious as he weighed what she'd said. "Okay," he answered finally. He took Nikki's hand and laced his fingers through hers. "I understand, I think. But that means *I'm* in on this, too."

He swung her hand as they walked to the door of their classroom, and Nikki felt her heart lift. She squeezed Tim's hand, silently thanking him. It was funny how, in the middle of so much trouble, she could find such happiness.

Robin had smiled all morning until her lips felt glued to her teeth. She could see the question in people's eyes as they wondered if she could be The One. All of that acting was exhausting her.

She tried to walk jauntily toward the cafeteria. The worst was still ahead of her: she had to see Cal during their lab period that afternoon. Robin was dreading that encounter. Would Calvin have heard? He was pretty much outside of the River Heights pipeline; he hated gossip. Maybe she'd be lucky.

Just ahead, Robin caught sight of a red-gold ponytail. Lacey. And was that Jeremy Pratt heading straight for her? Robin quickened her pace. Lacey couldn't stand Jeremy Pratt, and he wasn't fond of her, either.

Quickly Robin caught up to Lacey. "I thought you might need a bodyguard," she whispered.

"I can handle it," Lacey said through gritted teeth. "But thanks."

Jeremy approached casually, smoothing his multicolored Italian sweater, then said, "Well, Ms. Dupree, you're looking, ah—very demure and fetching today, very definitely fetching."

Lacey stared at him coolly. Robin had to admire her nerve.

Only a flicker of unease crossed Jeremy's face. Then he smiled. "I thought we could catch a movie tonight."

"Did you?" Lacey raised one eyebrow.

"Well, yeah. What do you say?" Jeremy leaned closer.

"I don't go to movies," Lacey replied.

"Oh." Jeremy shrugged. "Well, we could do something else. Leon's for pizza . . . Moon Lake . . ."

Lacey's pale blue eyes were frosty. "I don't eat pizza. And I hate lakes. All that algae. You know."

Jeremy looked confused. "Well, whatever you want, then. I'll call you—what's your phone number?"

"I don't have a phone." Lacey continued to meet his gaze steadily.

Jeremy looked blank. He laughed nervously.

"You don't have a phone?"

"I live in a log cabin," Lacey said. "And I never date people who aren't as smart as I am." She reached out and tapped him on the chest with her pencil. "Oh, yes. I also hate your sweater."

"Whoa," Jeremy said, stepping back. "Hey, excuse me for living."

"I'll think about it," Lacey told him. She pressed Robin's arm. Robin obediently speeded up her pace. Soon they'd left a dazed Jeremy Pratt far behind them.

"Wow," Robin said admiringly. "Can you teach me how to do that?"

Lacey frowned. "That Jeremy Pratt is a slime mold. He should be examined under a microscope."

They giggled together as they entered the cafeteria.

"Look, there's Nikki," Lacey said. "Why don't you two get lunch and I'll find us a table?"

"Sure," Robin said. "What would you like?"

"Anything," Lacey called as she moved away. "A sandwich."

Nikki came up and joined Robin. "Is everything okay?" she asked as they headed toward the line.

"Lacey just had a run-in with Mr. Preppie Pratt," Robin replied.

Nikki and Robin made their way to the end of the line. Absently, they chose sandwiches and drinks and pickles and chips. Nikki piled extra food on her tray for Lacey.

"Have you heard about the country club dance?" Nikki asked, trying to make conversation.

"Yes," Robin replied. "I guess I'll be going with Cal. We haven't talked about it, though, so maybe I'm not. If I do, I'll need a new dress. Maybe in a larger size."

"Stop it," Nikki said.

"Has Tim asked you yet?"

Nikki nodded. "This morning. Maybe you

and I should go shopping together tomorrow afternoon."

"I can't plan that far ahead," Robin said glumly. "I might be having a total collapse tomorrow."

Just then Robin noticed Kim Bishop and Samantha Daley in line in front of them. They had their heads together, whispering. "Watch out," she murmured. "Snob alert."

Kim twisted around. She glanced at Nikki's full tray. Then she turned back to Samantha.

"Maybe she's eating for two." The words floated back to Nikki and Robin clearly.

Nikki's chin lifted, and her blue eyes shone defiantly. She stared at Samantha's and Kim's backs as though she could make the two girls burst into flame.

But Robin's strength had suddenly drained away. That was the last straw. She knew she had to get out.

Abandoning her tray, Robin fled without a single word to Nikki. She pushed past the other students in line and walked quickly out of the cafeteria. Her face was burning as she made her way down the deserted hall. She didn't know where she was going; she just knew she had to get away.

The door to freedom was just down the stairs and around the corner. Robin needed to feel cool air on her face and in her hair.

She had to get out of River Heights High. She had to be alone.

Ready to sob with relief, Robin rounded the last corner and sprinted toward the double doors. Then she heard a voice.

"Robin! Hold on!"

7 〜

Robin stopped and waited for Calvin to catch up to her. "I was just going outside," she said.

"Outside?" Calvin asked, looking puzzled. "Aren't you supposed to be at lunch?"

"Do you always do what you're *supposed* to do, Calvin?"

A hurt look crossed his face, and Robin felt her heart constrict. What was making her say such awful things to him all the time? Maybe subconsciously she wanted him to go away until this mess was over. Or maybe, deep inside, she wanted him to make her tell him what was wrong. Because she did want to tell him so badly!

Before Robin could apologize, Calvin's expression changed. His mouth tightened and he took her firmly by the arm.

"You're coming with me," he told her. "Don't say no, don't say you can't, don't say you don't want to, don't say you don't have to. Because you do."

Robin nodded dazedly. She'd never seen Calvin like this before. She let him lead her outside. He started toward the bleachers.

"But, Cal——" she began.

"Be quiet," he ordered.

Robin sat down hard on the wooden bleachers. Calvin stood in front of her. But now that he had her there, he didn't seem to know how to begin.

"What's wrong with you, Robin?" Calvin finally burst out. "What's happening with us? Do you want to break up?" he demanded.

Mutely, Robin shook her head.

"Do you hate me?"

She shook her head again.

"Are you mad at me?"

Robin closed her eyes. "No," she said in a small voice.

Calvin squatted down in front of her. "Then what is it, Robin?"

She'd been right; he hadn't heard any

rumors yet. "Nothing." She looked down at the faded paint of the bleachers.

Calvin sat down next to her and sighed. "Robin," he said, staring at his clasped hands, "I know something's up. This isn't like you."

His tone was so gentle that Robin felt like crying. All she wanted was to throw herself into Calvin's arms and confess everything. Looking at his face, she felt love well up in her so sharply it made her catch her breath.

But she couldn't tell him. It wouldn't be fair. Not until she knew for sure. He'd worry needlessly and be unable to study. Calvin's grades were so important because he wanted to go to MIT, and he needed a scholarship to do it. Why should both of them flunk out?

"Come on," Calvin said. His sea green eyes were kind. "Tell me."

Robin turned away. She couldn't bear to see the tenderness in his eyes. "I told you, nothing's the matter," she said. "Except," she added, "that you keep asking me what's wrong."

It seemed to take an extra beat for her words to sink in. Then Calvin's face grew stony. "Fine," he said, jumping up. "If that's the way you want it. If you can't trust me, I don't see what we have together. If there was ever anything at all."

Calvin turned and walked quickly back to school. Robin had to force herself not to run after him. Tears filled her eyes and slipped down her cheeks. She told herself that everything would be all right. Calvin was hurt, so he'd said horrible things. Later she could explain to him why she'd kept silent, and he'd forgive her.

Robin stayed on the bench, hugging her knees. She was shaking badly now. Her thin jacket wasn't much protection against the brisk autumn wind. She really should go inside.

She stood up and looked over at the school. She'd rather die than go back in there. And how could she face lab period with Calvin now?

It was time to give up, Robin told herself. She was beaten by Brittany Tate, and she'd never been so frightened in her whole life. She wanted Calvin by her side now more than ever. Slowly Robin began to walk across the football field, away from school. Returning to classes was impossible. She hoped Lacey and Nikki would forgive her. A last sob broke from her, and Robin began to run.

Leon's was jammed. Brittany stood on her tiptoes and scanned the crowd. Finally she spotted Kim and Samantha in a back booth. She pushed through the crowd, exasperated. She had only a few minutes to relax before she had to take the bus to the mall and meet her mother at Blooms. She hated to work in the florist shop, and she didn't know why she had to. Her mother had a very capable assistant, Ruby. Couldn't they trim the roses or dump the daisies in pails without Brittany's help?

"Hey, what's up?" Samantha said as Brittany approached the table. "You look as pitiful as a little drowned kitten."

Kim shuddered. "Those southern expressions, Samantha. Really."

Brittany slid into the booth. "I'm fed up with the crowds," she said, waving a hand. She didn't want Kim to know she had to work that day. Kim had been so weird lately, and Brittany didn't want to give her any ammunition. "I'm used to the Westmoor hangouts now," she added breezily. "The college crowd is much more civilized."

Kim's eyes narrowed, and Brittany wondered if she'd made a mistake. She didn't have the energy to trade zingers with Kim now. Kim slumped back against her seat, and Brittany decided that she must be tired of all the nastiness, too.

"Brittany, have a slice of pizza," Samantha urged.

Brittany tried not to look at the pie in the

middle of the table. Fragrant, hot, bubbling with cheese and spicy tomato sauce — Leon's pizza pies were heaven. Her stomach growled. She'd dutifully spooned up a container of yogurt for lunch, and now she was starving. Telling Jack she loved sweets had been a big mistake. Yesterday he'd stopped off and bought her a pint of cookies 'n' cream ice cream on the way home, probably as a joke. Fortunately, Tamara and her father finished the ice cream in about three seconds flat.

"I'm not hungry," Brittany said. Her stomach growled again. She took a sip of diet soda and willed her stomach to behave itself.

Kim took a bite of pizza. "Mmmm," she said. "Worth every calorie." She wound a string of cheese around her tongue. "But this is definitely my last splurge for a while. I've got to squeeze into my new dress."

"You got a new dress?" Samantha asked.

Kim nodded. "Strapless. Taffeta. Midnight blue. Tiny little rhinestones sewn into the skirt. Deadly." She gave a languid shrug. "It was way too expensive, but it *is* for the country club dance. Are you going with Jack, Brittany?"

Zing. Brittany debated furiously with herself. She didn't even know there was going to be a dance; she wasn't a member of the club, and Jack hadn't mentioned it. Should she say she was going with him anyway? He'd probably ask her, but what if he didn't?

"We haven't talked about it yet," she said. "I'm seeing him tonight, though."

"Oh," Kim said. She paused. "Of course, so many of the college crowd are going that Jack might not want to be seen with someone still in high school. I mean, let's get real, Brittany. You've got some tough competition."

"I'm sure Brittany can handle it," Samantha said loyally.

"Oh, I'm sure she can, too," Kim said quickly, but the gleam in her frosty blue eyes said she wouldn't bet on it.

Brittany stood up. "Don't stay awake nights worrying, girls. Things are going just fine." She glanced at her watch. "Well, I'm out of here."

"Where are you going?" Kim asked. "It's not even four o'clock. Besides, we have to figure out which girl in Nikki's crowd is in trouble. Sam here thinks it's Robin, but I don't. *I* think it's Nikki. She and Tim Cooper are such a hot item."

Brittany felt a twinge of envy. It was obvious that Tim was crazy about Nikki, but Tim should have belonged to her, Brittany. She'd been cheated out of him and made to confess to a scheme she'd had to discredit Nikki.

At first she thought it was Nikki who had blackmailed her, but now she was sure it was Robin or Lacey. And for the last couple of weeks, she'd suspected Lacey. There was something about the way the Mouse had looked at her in the first couple of days after Tim had gone back to Nikki. Her usual spacey expression seemed to have a steel edge to it.

"Personally, I think it's sweet little Lacey Dupree," Brittany said.

Samantha and Kim traded surprised glances. Then they nodded slowly, trying out the idea.

"Now I really have to run," Brittany said. "Jack's going to call me at four-thirty."

She swept out of Leon's, tossing her head to each admiring glance, responding with a smile and a teasing comment to every hello. But deep inside her a small, desperate anxiety was growing.

The country club dance was the biggest event of the season. If she was there on Jack Reilly's arm, even Nikki Masters would be eclipsed. He *had* to take her to the dance. He had to.

"Hi, honey, you're finally here," Mrs. Tate greeted her. "Great. Can you fill those white buckets over there with water? I just got a delivery of cornflowers. Ruby will show you how to bunch them. Oh, and then I'd like you to arrange some bouquets." Her mother smiled. "Here, wear this apron so you don't get that pretty sweater all wet."

Brittany sighed and tied the horrid stained apron around her waist. She dutifully picked up the buckets and headed to the sink in the back room. "Hi, Ruby," she said to her mother's assistant.

Ruby Chang looked up from arranging an elaborate display of exotic blooms and pushed her thick black bangs out of her eyes. "Hi, sweetie. It's terrific of you to come help us out. We're really swamped today."

"Glad to do it," Brittany said. She started to fill the buckets with water. How she hated working! If only her mother would give up her business.

Her mother grinned at her over an armload of flowers, her face flushed and pretty. For some reason, her mother got so much satisfaction out of working. And, Brittany grudgingly admitted, Blooms wasn't a run-of-the-mill florist shop, either. Ruby was a genius at unusual floral arrangements, and everyone agreed her mother had excellent taste. The shop had quite a good reputation.

Brittany dragged the first bucket of cornflowers to the front of the shop. Then she looked through the front window to check out the action at the mall. To her horror, she saw Jack Reilly about ten yards away.

Instinctively, Brittany ducked. Luckily, there was a jungle of plants at the front of the shop. Jack hadn't seen her, thank heavens. She peered out through the leaves of a large ficus plant.

Jack was standing with a group of college kids. One of the girls, a tall redhead, was laughing with him.

Brittany let out her breath in a sharp hiss. Here she was, stuck in this stupid store, and some other girl was moving in! What if Jack asked *her* to the dance? She watched as the redhead looked over at Blooms, said something to Jack, and touched his shoulder. They started to move toward the store.

With a muffled cry, Brittany began to scuttle backward on her hands and knees. They were going to come in! Still using the plants as cover, she turned and crawled as fast as she could toward the back room.

She rounded the desk, still on her hands and knees. Her mother's jaw dropped.

"Hi," Brittany said, crawling past her. The bell on the front door jangled.

"I guess I'll take care of it," her mother said, sounding confused. "Are you all right?"

Brittany nodded quickly and made a shooing motion with her hands. "Go ahead," she whispered.

As Mrs. Tate went to wait on the customers, Brittany melted back into the shadows against the wall. When she heard a middle-aged woman asking for chrysanthemums, she peered around the desk.

There was no sign of Jack. Standing up and craning her neck, Brittany could see through the front window that he had drifted off with the crowd to the bookstore.

Slowly her heartbeat returned to normal. She glanced down at herself and sighed. There was a hole in the left knee of her new black tights, and her denim miniskirt had a smear of dirt across the front.

Brittany slumped into a chair. Her stomach growled. She rested her chin in her hands and discovered that she was developing a pimple in the middle of it from all that chocolate. She sighed again heavily. Was Jack Reilly really worth it?

8

When the phone rang, Robin jumped. Maybe it was Calvin, wanting to make up.

"Hello?" she said breathlessly.

"Robin, it's Nikki. What happened to you today?"

Robin flopped back on the pillows of her bed. "I, uh, left school."

"You *left?*"

"I couldn't take it anymore, Nikki. I'm sorry. I really appreciate what you and Lacey did, and I know it was especially hard for you. Do you forgive me?"

"Forgive you? For what? Robin, I don't

care what anybody at school says. I'm worried about *you*. Why did you leave like that?"

Robin picked at her chenille bedspread. "Oh, I had a million reasons."

"Name one."

"Kim Bishop," Robin shot back.

"That's not good enough."

Robin flopped over, groaning. She knew Nikki wouldn't give up. "Calvin Roth."

"Aha. What happened with Cal?"

"We broke up."

"What happened?" Nikki asked.

Robin sighed. "Well, he asked me what was wrong, and I said nothing, and he said if I didn't trust him there was no use being together. Please don't say I told you so. I just couldn't tell him."

"Oh, Robin," Nikki said. "I'm so sorry. What did you do with yourself all afternoon?"

"Nothing," Robin answered. "I walked around for a while. Then I got cold, so I went to the mall. I sat in the Burger Boy until they kicked me out. Then I walked home."

There was a pause. Then Nikki spoke softly. "Don't you think this has gone far enough, Robin?"

Robin rolled over again. "Yes, I guess so."

"Don't you think it's time you proved to

yourself that you're not pregnant?" Nikki
went on. "You're torturing yourself."

Sighing, Robin wound the phone cord
around her finger. "You're right."

"Good," Nikki said, sounding relieved.
"Listen, I found out about this women's
health clinic downtown. They do free exams,
and tests. You'd hear the good news from an
authority figure in a white coat, remember?
It's a very respected clinic. I read an article
about it in the library."

Robin hesitated. "That was nice of you,
Nikki."

"So you'll go?"

"Yes. I'll go." Robin felt fear snake
through her. She *would* go. It was time to be
responsible and stop running away. She'd
upset her friends, and she'd already hurt
Calvin enough.

"Well, that's great," Nikki said brightly.
"Because I, uh, made an appointment for
you. They can fit you in tomorrow, isn't that
terrific? And Lacey and I will go with you.
Okay?"

"Nikki, it sounds like a good idea," Robin
said slowly. "But I can't go tomorrow."

Nikki sounded annoyed. "Do you have
something better to do?"

"No, it's not that," Robin replied. "The
school called about my taking off today, and
my parents had a fit. Then they really hit the

ceiling when I told them I flunked my history test. I can't go anywhere all weekend. I'm grounded."

"Grounded for the weekend!" Nikki exclaimed. "You've got to be kidding!"

"I wish," Robin said. "But it's a royal decree. Handed down from on high — my father's study. It was a pretty ugly scene. Be glad you weren't there."

"I can't believe they were that angry," Nikki said.

"Actually, right now they're pretty worried about me. I'd almost rather they yelled and screamed."

Nikki thought for a moment. "Hmmm. Maybe I can change the appointment to next Saturday."

"Thanks for doing this, Nikki," Robin said.

"No problem," Nikki replied. "So what are you going to do all weekend, Rob?"

Robin laughed shortly. "Besides sulk, you mean? Well, my little brother felt sorry for me, so he offered me his videos. I've got a shelf full of cartoons to watch. What a wild weekend!"

Nikki laughed. "Can you have visitors, at least? Lacey has to work, but I can come over."

"Great!" Robin said. "You could pay a visit to the prisoner on Saturday afternoon, if you want. My social calendar is absolutely blank, darling."

Nikki giggled. "Ta-ta," she said.

After school on Monday Brittany lay on her bed, her chin in her hands. The weekend had been a dud. The only thing she'd been able to think about was the country club dance. Even her Saturday night date with Jack had been spoiled by her waiting for him to ask her. She had looked gorgeous in her red minidress—even Tamara had said so. She was bright and bubbly all night, even though she hadn't understood the boring play Jack had taken her to. She'd kissed him good night and clung to him for a long moment before pulling away, but still he hadn't mentioned the dance.

It was torture to have to wait like this. Brittany had never been patient, but it had never mattered so much before. If on the off-chance the boy she liked didn't ask her out, she went with someone else. But this time she didn't want to go to the dance with anyone but Jack.

Brittany sighed. While she waited for Jack to make his move, every decent guy in school was being snatched up. Samantha was going with Avery Glass. Kim was going with Erik Nielson. And, of course, Tim Cooper was taking Nikki. Pretty soon, she wouldn't be able to go to the dance at all!

Brittany quickly ran over the remaining candidates in her mind. Then she sat up with a start. Hadn't Calvin Roth and Robin Fisher broken up? He was quiet, but definitely cute and smart. Brittany's lips curved in a soft, delighted smile. If Jack Reilly didn't ask her, she'd have a consolation prize.

Wednesday. A perfectly fine day, with history and English in the morning and study hall right after lunch. A free period in the afternoon. The only thing wrong with Wednesday, Brittany told herself, was that it was only three days away from Saturday. And that rat Jack *still* hadn't asked her to the country club dance!

Brittany sat in the library, pretending to study. She was beginning to despair. This was the first time she was giving a guy extra time to ask her.

In the cafeteria Brittany had been sure she would lose her lunch if Kim said one more syllable about her midnight blue taffeta dress. Samantha had joined in the chorus, bragging about *her* new dress. Outside Brittany had remained lofty and unconcerned, but inside, she was a mess. Instead of sitting with her friends in study hall, Brittany had gone to the library to be alone.

Did Jack think she was too young? Or was he finally put off by her ordinary family? On Monday night Tamara had been downstairs again, hanging around and making eyes at him. Jack still hadn't met her mother. Brittany always made sure he picked her up before Mrs. Tate arrived home so there would be no danger of his finding out about Blooms. Brittany was getting tired of inventing imaginary committees for her mother to serve on.

Maybe Jack wasn't asking her to the dance because he'd found out that the Tates didn't belong to the club. Or maybe he was one of those guys who just *assumed* they'd be going together? Brittany's dark eyes flashed.

Only one more chance, Brittany vowed, ducking her head over her book. If Jack didn't ask her that very day, she'd start working on Calvin Roth. Compared to Jack, he'd be a snap.

Brittany dawdled at her locker until she was sure everybody would be outside. She wanted every single person at River Heights High to see Jack's sports car.

And they did. Everyone stopped and stared as Brittany casually made her way to the car. Then Jack actually got out and walked around the car to open the passenger door. Brittany could almost feel every girl in the crowd swoon.

Jack slid into the driver's seat. "You look terrific," he said. "Here. I brought you a present." He handed her a small gold-foil box of French chocolates.

"Oh, Jack. How sweet. Thank you." Brittany smiled, even though she felt like pitching the box at his head. Maybe this was a conspiracy. Someone had hired Jack Reilly to make her fat. Nikki Masters, no doubt.

Suddenly Brittany had an idea. She shook the box of chocolates at him playfully. "If you keep this up, I won't fit into any of my dresses." She'd always had a strict rule about not talking about her weight in front of guys—they hated that kind of thing. In this case, though, it might be useful.

"Oh, I don't think you have to worry much," Jack said with a smile.

"But I have a brand-new dress," Brittany went on. "And it's, well, pretty formfitting," she added.

"Maybe I should bring you someplace to wear that new dress," Jack suggested, putting his hand on the ignition key, but not turning it.

Finally! Brittany cocked a flirtatious eyebrow. "Oh?" she said.

Tap, tap, tap. Brittany twisted around and stifled a groan. Tamara was standing right outside the car. Brittany rolled her window down.

"What are you doing here?" she demanded irritably. Her sister was in junior high, which was a couple of blocks away.

Tamara leaned in and ignored Brittany completely. "Hi, Jack. I'm on the way to the mall, but the bus is late. Do you think you could give me a ride?"

"Sure, kiddo," Jack replied. "Climb in."

"Sit in the back seat, Tamara," Brittany said. But the twerp was already opening the door and sliding onto the front seat, pushing Brittany over toward the stick shift.

"Britty, move," Tamara said. "Hey, what are these, chocolates? Oh, give them to me." She turned to Jack. "Britty never eats—"

"Tamara," Brittany broke in smoothly, "if I let you sit in the front seat, will you be quiet? Jack and I were having a conversation."

Tamara shrugged. "Sure."

Sighing, Brittany slipped through the seats and landed awkwardly in the back. Her foot hit the stick shift.

"Careful, Britty," Tamara said.

Brittany prayed that Jack wouldn't pick up on that odious nickname. She felt like screaming, but she settled into the seat without a word. She drew her legs up and tried to look serene, in case Jack glanced at her in the rearview mirror.

"Wow, this is a neat car," Tamara piped up. "Have you had it long? What year is it?"

For the rest of the ride, Brittany stared out the window as River Heights passed by and Jack and Tamara chattered about Jack's car.

Brittany smiled sourly. Tamara had sure zeroed in on the subject closest to every guy's heart: his car. The little weasel! Brittany sighed. Tamara had just proved without a doubt that she was Brittany Tate's younger sister, after all.

9

"This is ridiculous," Robin grumbled as she whipped through a rack of dresses. "I'm not going to the dance. Why are we even here?"

"You *are* going to the dance," Nikki answered calmly. "You're not grounded anymore, are you?"

"No, that was just last weekend. But I'm still in the doghouse," Robin said. "If I come back a second past five today, I'll be grounded for a week."

"We won't be late." Nikki rejected a frothy blue dress and held up a wild fuschia chiffon with a pleated bodice. "How about this one?"

Robin considered it. "Maybe. It doesn't matter anyway. I'm not going to the dance, Nikki. The only time I've seen Cal is in lab. I stare at him through my plastic goggles. And all he says are things like 'Pass the potassium.'"

Nikki thrust the dress at her. "Try it on, Robin. Look," she said under her breath, "we made the appointment. On Saturday, you'll know for sure. That's only three days away. You'll get the good news, and you'll make up with Cal at the dance." She frowned. "You'd better have a killer dress, though. He's probably still going to be pretty mad." She brightened. "Besides, you'll have something to celebrate."

"Like what?" Robin grumbled. "Going to a dance all by myself?"

"Cal will be going alone, too," Nikki told her. "Maybe you'll make it up with him by then."

"Right," Robin said. "And maybe Brittany Tate will apologize for spreading nasty rumors and be my best friend."

"Robin—" Nikki started.

"Okay, okay." Robin paused. "Kim Bishop?"

Nikki shook a frilly peach gown at her. "If you don't behave yourself, I'll make you wear this. You should be grateful that the dance is the new topic of conversation at school."

Robin sighed. "You're right. I should be optimistic. But I really don't think I'll be going to that dance."

Nikki gave her a sidelong glance. "Not even if you had *this* to wear?" She paused dramatically, then held up another dress that she knew Robin would love. It was a deep purple lace minidress over an underskirt of acid green. It was also extremely short, chic, and sexy.

Robin gasped. "You're torturing me!" She took the dress from Nikki gingerly, as if it might bite her. "Well, I might as well try it on," she said. "Just for fun. I don't have to buy it."

"No, of course not." Nikki smiled. She knew that once Robin tried the dress on, she wouldn't be able to resist it.

As they passed the window of the boutique, on their way to the dressing room, Robin glanced out and saw Brittany Tate drifting by on the arm of a tall, good-looking guy. They were heading toward the ice-cream parlor across the mall. "Don't look now, but it's Brittany and that new boyfriend of hers," Robin said. "What's his name again?"

Nikki peeked out. "Jack Reilly."

Robin shook her head. "I'll never forget that scene in the drugstore as long as I live." She gripped Nikki's arm. "That reminds me. What if someone sees us go into the clinic?"

"Nobody will see us," Nikki said.

"That's what you said about the drugstore," Robin reminded her.

"But the clinic is downtown, in the business district," Nikki said. "Nobody we know goes down there."

Robin bit her lip. "Do you know *exactly* where it is?" she persisted.

Nikki was beginning to look annoyed. "Robin, we'll find it, okay? How hard can it be?" She pulled Robin toward the dressing room. "Come on."

Robin clutched the dress against her. "I know," she said. "We'll have a trial run. We can drive down after school tomorrow. No, on Friday, I have swim practice tomorrow. That way, we'll be prepared."

"All right," Nikki said soothingly. "If that's what you want to do."

Robin smiled. "Thanks, Nikki. You're a pal."

"Now stop worrying," Nikki said.

"I can't help it." Robin looked back over her shoulder. Brittany Tate was walking by again with Jack. Both of them were balancing huge plastic dishes full of ice cream and whipped cream. "Look at her!" Robin said disgustedly. "She practically destroys our lives, and she's laughing. She's eating a hot fudge sundae, like she's the happiest person in the world."

Brittany kept a smile on her face, but inside she was seething. Jack hadn't actually brought up the dance yet, and she refused to keep hinting. And he'd insisted on buying her this gross hot fudge sundae. Not only did she have to eat it, she had to carry it around as they walked! Everyone would think she was a pig.

At least Tamara wasn't around. Brittany had made sure her sister headed off with her friends as soon as they'd arrived.

Jack scooped up a heaping spoonful of gooey butterscotch and fed some to Brittany. She dimpled prettily.

"Mmmm. Delicious," she said. "Why don't we sit down by the fountain over there?"

"Sure," Jack replied.

Brittany picked a bench where the over-hanging palms would give them privacy.

"So," Jack said as they settled themselves, "how is your dad doing these days?"

"My father? Oh, much better." Brittany looked at him shyly. "Thanks to you."

Jack grinned. "I was glad to do it. And my

project is turning out fine, after all." He paused. "The only bad thing was that it cut down on the amount of time I could spend with you." He squeezed her hand meaningfully.

Brittany looked down at her sundae. "You don't mean that."

"Hey, don't you trust me?" Jack asked with a gleam in his eye.

No, Brittany told him silently. "I'm not sure if I do or not," she said aloud. She felt a pulse beating in her throat.

Jack took her ice cream and put it down next to his on the bench. "Well," he said lightly, "what are we going to do about this? You seem to be afraid of me."

Brittany jerked her head back. "I'm not afraid of you, Jack Reilly!"

Jack laughed. "Then why don't you trust me, Brittany?"

"Because I don't know how you feel!" she burst out. Then her mouth dropped open in horror. She'd broken another one of her rules! Never, *ever*, tell a guy what you really think.

Jack gave a soft laugh, but somehow Brittany didn't mind it this time. There was no mockery in it. He brushed a strand of dark hair away from her cheek. "Oh, Brittany," he said. "You're right. Maybe I joke around too much sometimes. Maybe I'm the one who's afraid of you."

That was more like it. Brittany ducked her head. She heard a small rustle in the leaves behind her, but Jack was on her favorite subject now. He was close to asking her to the dance. She could feel it.

"You know, I'm a little embarrassed," Jack began. "There's something I keep meaning to ask you. I guess when I'm with you I start thinking about other things, or we get interrupted—"

There was another rustle behind them. Brittany hoped there weren't mice in the palms. What if it was a rat? Brittany focused carefully on Jack. No creature on earth was going to interrupt *this* scene!

"I know it's Wednesday already," Jack went on. "But—"

Brittany jumped. "Oh, no!" she gasped. Over Jack's left shoulder, two dark eyes were peering out of the shrubbery.

"No?" Jack asked, confused. "I didn't even ask you yet."

But Brittany barely heard him. She leaped up and jumped onto the seat. Reaching past Jack, she tried to grab Tamara's ponytail.

"Come here," she screeched. "You snooping little—"

Tamara leaned back, and Brittany's hand

met empty air. Then Tamara's sneaker slipped on the wet edge of the fountain, and over she went. With a loud splash, she fell into the shallow pool. Water flew into Brittany's face and down her neck.

Jack jumped up and climbed over the vegetation. "Tamara, are you okay?" he asked anxiously.

Brittany fished in her purse for her handkerchief. Tamara was fine. She might never walk again, though, once Brittany was through with her.

Jack picked Tamara up in his arms. Water streamed down his sweater. Tamara looked as though she were about to melt. Brittany hoped she was happy. Everyone should be happy in their last moments on earth.

Jack deposited the sopping Tamara next to Brittany. He was laughing.

"What a sight the two of you are," he said.

Brittany glared at Tamara. "What are you doing here?" she demanded.

Tamara shrugged. "I came with you, remember? I'm supposed to meet Mom later at the sh—"

"Well, first you're coming with me." Brittany grabbed Tamara's arm. "I'm going to clean you up in the rest room, sweetie. I wouldn't want you to catch cold," she added tenderly.

"Be right back, Jack," Tamara said over her shoulder.

"No, you won't," Brittany told her through clenched teeth. "Now, come on, sister dear. We've got some talking to do."

For once, everything turned out just the way Brittany wanted. Tamara agreed, after numerous threats, to leave her and Jack alone. She went happily off to Blooms, and Brittany didn't see a trace of her for the rest of the afternoon.

And, after apologizing for asking so late, Jack finally invited her to the dance. He kissed her goodbye lingeringly and promised to call her later. It was almost as though her one flash of honesty had made him like her more. Now, that was interesting.

She couldn't wait to see the look on Kim's face at school the next day. No, she wouldn't tell her, Brittany decided. She'd wait until Kim asked.

Brittany sat dreaming at the dinner table, not listening to any of the conversation around her. She toyed with her mashed potatoes, thinking about the fantastic new dress she would have to buy. She had only three shopping days left.

Suddenly two words caught Brittany's attention. She sat up.

Country club. Her mother was talking about the country club dance?

"I hear it's very la-di-da," Mrs. Tate was saying. "And since it's at the club, we might get more jobs there in the future. I'm sorry the other florist shop burned down, of course, but this could be a real break for Blooms."

"It sounds great, Susan," Mr. Tate said.

"Congratulations, Mom," Tamara said.

"I don't have the job yet, honey," Mrs. Tate told Tamara, "but I did put in a bid. The board has to decide tomorrow, though, to give us time to order our shipments. It will be a terrible rush." She turned to Mr. Tate. "Have some potatoes, dear."

"You mean you might get the contract for the country club dance?" Brittany asked.

"Oh, I hope so, honey," her mother replied.

"Who are you up against?" Brittany asked. She felt very nervous all of a sudden.

"Flowers by Antoine," Mrs. Tate replied. "You know—that expensive florist downtown. We're much better than he is, if I do say so myself. He'll just throw around some fall mums in yellows and oranges."

"What would you do, Mom?" Tamara asked.

"Oh, Ruby and I came up with some terrific ideas. We thought we'd float gardenias in bowls. And white irises and some lilies of the valley at the tables. Not masses of flowers, just delicate arrangements. Everything would be white, with touches of green and gold. What do you think?

"Lovely." Brittany gulped.

Mrs. Tate pushed her plate away, her dark eyes shining. "I'm so excited about this project. It would be the most important contract I've ever had. I'm going to make sure every little detail is absolutely perfect."

A horrible certainty began to dawn on Brittany. "What do you mean, Mom?"

"Well, I'm going to have to go to the club that night. Not one petal on my flowers will be wilted. I'm going to be there myself to make sure of it!"

Brittany almost fainted. Her *mother* was going to the dance! Everyone would see her. She closed her eyes, picturing Kim's glee as Mrs. Tate fussed among the tables. Now it didn't matter how gorgeous Brittany looked that night. She'd be related to the hired help!

10 ~~~

Brittany had to have a plan, but she didn't have much time. The club wasn't big enough for both her and her mom, and Brittany knew *she* wasn't going to be the one to stay home.

She came into the kitchen the next morning full of purpose. As she grabbed a banana for breakfast, her mother made her sleepy way to the coffeepot. Mrs. Tate always had a hard time waking up.

"Mom, how do you figure out a bid, exactly?"

Mrs. Tate looked at her over the coffeepot,

bleary-eyed. "Why are you asking me this question before I'm awake?"

"Oh, sorry," Brittany said quickly. "I was just thinking about it, I guess."

"It's nice that you're taking an interest in the business, honey," Mrs. Tate said, pouring herself a cup of coffee. She took a long sip. "The next time you come to work, I'll explain it all to you. I'll have to show you figures and estimates and labor costs. The whole shebang."

"Thanks, I'd like that." Brittany took a bite of her banana. On her next workday she was in for one boring afternoon, that was for sure. "But I was just wondering about really big jobs. Like this one for the country club, for instance."

In the next ten minutes, Brittany learned more than she had ever wanted to know about bidding problems for a small business. But it worked. Her mother actually told her the amount of her bid. Then she told Brittany to eat something more than a banana and returned upstairs, the sash of her robe trailing behind her.

Brittany smiled a secret smile of satisfaction. Step One completed. Now for Step Two.

"Are you satisfied, Robin?" Nikki asked, pulling the car over to the curb. "There's the clinic. It has a huge parking lot. We made it here in exactly fifteen minutes."

"And it's Friday, so there's even more traffic," Lacey added. "Saturday will be a breeze."

"Thanks, guys," Robin said. "I really—" Suddenly she slid off her seat and dropped to the floor.

Nikki frowned. "Robin?"

"Shhhh," Robin hissed. She pointed frantically toward the outside of the car. "Brittany!"

"What?" Nikki scanned the sidewalk.

"Behind you!" Robin whispered.

Nikki glanced in the rearview mirror, and Lacey twisted around in her seat. Sure enough, there was Brittany Tate, getting off a bus. She was looking around as though she might be lost.

"Get down!" Robin told them.

"I wonder what Brittany's doing here," Lacey said.

"She's spying on us! She knows! Hide!" Robin said wildly.

"I don't think so," Nikki said slowly, watching Brittany cross the street. "She can't see us, Robin."

"She *followed* us!" Robin insisted.

"How could she follow us on a bus?" Lacey asked reasonably. "Maybe she's meeting Jack Reilly down here. Why would she want to trail around after us, anyway?"

"You're asking that question about Brittany Tate?" Robin wailed. "Nikki, let's go."

"Hold on," Nikki said. "If I pull out now, she might see us. Let's just hang out a second."

"I knew we should have worn disguises," Robin moaned.

"She's going into the florist shop down the street," Nikki ·said with satisfaction. "She wasn't looking for us at all. The coast is clear." She started the car. "We're all set for tomorrow, Robin. This time nothing will stop us!"

Flowers by Antoine was in a part of River Heights Brittany didn't know very well. She hadn't been sure which way to go. She walked several blocks before she discovered that the numbers were going the wrong way. Exasperated, she turned around and started up again.

Finally, she noticed a striped awning and stepped up her pace. Antoine's looked like a very classy florist. Her spirits lifted. Maybe her mother had downplayed the shop. Maybe Antoine would win the bid without any help from Brittany.

But how could she be sure? Straightening her shoulders, Brittany opened the door.

She took a deep, perfumed breath. It was a nice shop, but she could tell immediately that the flowers weren't as fresh, the arrangements as daring as Blooms. She felt a small flush of pride in her mother.

A fussy-looking little man came out from the back of the shop. "May I help you, young lady?"

"Perhaps," Brittany said, putting on her most aristocratic air. She imitated Kim's casual posture as she surveyed the flowers with a critical eye. Finally she turned back to the man.

"It's a lovely shop," she said. "My father told me to stop in."

"Your father is one of my customers?" the man asked.

Brittany looked prettily confused. "Oh, are you Antoine?"

"Yes, I am," he replied.

She laughed lightly. "Oh, I'm sorry. It's just that—well, I expected a younger man from my father's description. He buys flowers here quite often. And he's on the country club board."

"I see. His name?"

"You have some lovely chrysanthemums," Brittany said. "A misunderstood flower, don't you agree?" She fixed her dark eyes on the little man. She had no idea what she was talking about. But if Monsieur Antoine agreed with her, she had him.

"Yes, yes, I agree," Antoine said quickly. "Exactly. How beautifully put—a misunderstood flower, yes. And here, I have some lovely roses. Sterling silver roses, very special."

"Lovely," Brittany said. "Oh, I *do* hope you do the flowers at the dance! You have such an artistic eye."

"Thank you," Antoine replied. "I, too, hope to do the dance this weekend."

Brittany sighed and bent to sniff a bouquet. "How unfortunate that— Oh, well."

"There is some problem?" Antoine frowned.

"No, no. Well, yes." Brittany stepped closer. She had to force herself not to step back again when she caught a whiff of his aftershave. Ugh. "Even the country club has to be careful with funds," she went on. "They want artistry, and yet—" She sighed. "They're not willing to pay. And from what my father told me of the bids, well—"

"I see. Here, allow me to make a gift to you of these lovely sterling silver roses." Antoine presented Brittany with three roses. Then he leaned closer. Brittany couldn't help it; that time she actually did step back.

"Perhaps," Antoine said, "perhaps you

would know approximately what the other bid would be?"

Here was the moment. It would be so simple. Just a discreet word in the right place. Her specialty.

"Because one can always adjust a bid, you know," Antoine added conspiratorially.

Brittany smiled weakly. She found herself smack up against a problem she hadn't anticipated—loyalty.

She knew, right then, that she couldn't do it. She couldn't sabotage her mother's bid. No matter how much it might hurt her with Jack.

"I wouldn't have the slightest idea," Brittany said coolly. "But good luck." Clutching her roses and leaving Antoine open-mouthed behind her, she fled the shop. After a block she dumped the flowers into a trash can.

Brittany made her way toward the back of the bus. It was crowded with rush-hour passengers, and she had to squeeze her way into an empty space by a pole. She needed to think.

She had to come up with another plan. She needed something that would prevent her mother from going to the club but wouldn't prevent Blooms from winning the contract.

It wasn't until she reached her stop that

she knew what she was going to do. Like most perfect plans, it was simple. She flew off the bus with a dazzling smile for the bus driver.

By the time Brittany reached her front door, she had figured out every detail. She felt positively cheerful as she entered the kitchen.

Mrs. Tate was taking a chicken out of the oven. "Oh, you're home. Good. Dinner's almost ready. Can you set the table, Brittany?"

"Sure." She began to take out knives and forks from the drawer. "Mom, I've been thinking. I'd really like to help you with this country club thing when you get the contract. You know, take over some of the work at the shop so you and Ruby can really concentrate."

"That's sweet of you, Brittany, but I think we'll have everything under control."

Brittany's brain whirred in confusion. She hadn't expected her mother to refuse her offer. She'd imagined that her mother would practically fall on her knees in shock and appreciation. "I could come in for a few hours on Saturday," Brittany suggested. "I wouldn't mind, really."

"Aren't you going to the dance, dear?" Mrs. Tate asked. "You won't want to work that day. I know how you like to get ready—take a bath, do your hair. And you haven't even bought a dress yet.''

"Oh, I'll have plenty of time tomorrow," Brittany assured her. Since when did her mother try to talk her out of working at the shop? She put her hand on her mother's shoulder. "I'd really like to help you, Mom," she said earnestly.

Mrs. Tate looked pleased. "Isn't that nice. Well, if you really want to, dear. You can come in in the morning and leave after lunch. That should give you enough time to buy a dress and get ready." She gave Brittany a slightly perplexed smile. "This is very sweet of you.''

"I just want to help out," Brittany said, carefully placing the knives on the table. Plan B was in motion.

11

On Saturday morning Robin awoke to a cool, clear day. But as soon as she opened her eyes, she felt sick.

"Nerves," Robin said out loud. She looked over at her closet. Her new dress hung on the doorknob. Nikki had been right. There *was* life beyond her appointment at eleven-thirty. Things might even turn out okay.

She showered and dressed carefully in her best underwear. Then she pulled on a pair of soft faded jeans and her lucky sweater. As a final touch she added a slouchy black hat and sunglasses.

Robin looked in the mirror. She had

thought she'd look mysterious, but she didn't. She looked just like Robin Fisher in a hat and sunglasses.

Nikki pulled up to her door at exactly eleven-ten. Both she and Lacey were wearing hats and sunglasses, as Robin had requested.

"I feel ridiculous," Lacey said. Her baseball cap was pulled down low on her forehead, hiding her red hair.

"Me, too," Nikki agreed. She was wearing a gray fedora.

"I think you both look great," Robin told them, sliding into the back seat. "Nobody will recognize us now."

Lacey and Nikki traded glances. In Nikki's metallic blue Camaro, they weren't exactly inconspicuous.

"I guess we should be grateful you didn't want us to rent a car," Nikki said.

"I thought about it," Robin said absently as she twisted around to check out the quiet street behind them. "But we're too young."

The streets were quiet, and to Robin, they seemed to arrive at the clinic in seconds. Before she knew what was happening, she was getting out of the car. With Nikki and Lacey flanking her, she walked quickly around the building to the front entrance. But when she saw the door in front of her, Robin hesitated.

"We're with you all the way," Nikki said.

"All the way," Lacey repeated.

They went inside. There were only about three other girls in the waiting room, all of them older than Robin.

Nikki, Lacey, and Robin went up to the desk together. A gray-haired woman with a kind, lined face looked up.

"I'm Robin Fisher," Robin said. Her voice sounded weak. She tried again. "Fisher. I have an appointment at eleven-thirty."

The woman consulted a list. "Yes, Robin. I'd like you to fill this out." She handed her a clipboard with a long white form on it. "Why don't you and your friends take a seat and we'll call you. Bring this up when you're through. If you don't understand a question, leave it blank."

They found seats together. Lacey and Nikki picked up magazines, and Robin bent over the form and began to fill in the information. She was glad to have something to do.

She squinted uneasily at the questions. "Do you guys think I have a nervous condition?" she whispered.

"No," Lacey and Nikki answered in unison.

Robin finished filling out the form and returned it to the desk. A woman in a white

coat came out and called, "April Downing?"
One of the girls got up and went into the back
office.

Robin took a deep breath. Her heart was
pounding, and her palms were slick with
sweat. She'd never been more nervous in her
life.

Maybe she could just sit here forever,
Robin thought dazedly. Maybe they'd never
call her name. Maybe they'd lost her form.

"Robin Fisher?"

She vaulted out of her seat. "Here! Present!" Everyone in the waiting room looked
up, and Robin flushed. The woman in the
white coat smiled. "I mean, hi," Robin said.
With a last despairing look at Nikki and
Lacey, she went through the door.

When Mrs. Tate won the contract, Brittany
discovered that there was an advantage to
having your mother do the flower arrangements for a big dance after all. She knew
what the color scheme would be. So as soon
as she saw the dress, she knew it was the
right one. She didn't have to look any further.

The dress was white, a creamy confection
in velvet and chiffon. Normally, Brittany
would have flipped right past it. Who would
wear white to a fall dance? But that was the
beauty of it. Against the gardenias and white

irises her mother was using for her theme, it would be perfect.

Twisting in the dressing room mirror to see herself from all angles, Brittany pictured herself shimmering like moonlight amid all the busy reds and bright blues of the other girls. Brittany smiled slowly. If she wanted to stand out, if she wanted to look classy, this dress would do it.

Quickly she brought it to the saleswoman to ring up. She had to get back to Blooms. She'd come to work with her mother at ten, and so far all she'd done was shop. She'd said she'd be back in half an hour, but prowling the stores had taken much of the morning.

Brittany raced to Blooms, her dress trailing behind her like a banner in its bright red garment bag.

"Sorry, Mom," she said when she reached the flower shop. "The lines were so long, but I got the most perfect dress."

Mrs. Tate looked up with a bright smile. "That's all right, honey. Ruby and I have things under control. Let me see the dress. Oooh, that's lovely. You'll look just beautiful. And it will go so beautifully with the gardenias and white irises."

"That's what I thought." Brittany felt pleased.

"I'll tell you what," Mrs. Tate said. "Do you want to wear my gold evening coat?"

"Oh, could I?" Brittany asked breathily.

Mrs. Tate laughed. "Of course. I can't wait to see you there tonight."

Smiling, Brittany went to the back room to hang up her dress. It was too bad her mother wouldn't get to see her at the club. If her mother wanted to see Brittany at the country club, she should get her husband to join it.

Robin sat shivering on the edge of the padded table. The examination was over in minutes. It had been painless and fast, but she couldn't stop her knees from shaking. The doctor, who told Robin to call her Annamarie, had been very nice about the whole thing. She said that most girls were nervous during the exam. It was lucky for everyone it was so short.

Robin's paper smock had rivers of perspiration running down it, but her feet felt like two ice cubes in her damp orange socks.

Annamarie patted Robin's knee. Her hand was warm and dry. "You can get dressed now, Robin. It's going to take a few minutes to complete the test. Why don't you go back to the waiting room, and I'll call you?"

Robin nodded.

Annamarie smiled reassuringly. She had dark hair threaded with silver, and she wore no makeup. Her blue eyes looked intelligent

and kind. "I'll come and get you as soon as I
know," she said. "Don't worry," she added.
"We're here to help."

The doctor left, closing the door softly
behind her. Robin slid off the table and
dressed quickly, jumping a little when her
cold fingers came in contact with bare skin.

Nikki and Lacey looked up expectantly
when she came out. Robin shook her head
ruefully as she crossed the room.

"I don't know yet," she said in a low tone.
"I'm supposed to wait out here until the
doctor calls me back in."

More waiting. Nikki and Lacey turned
back to their magazines. Robin sat hunched
over in her seat, clasping and unclasping her
hands.

After what seemed like an hour, Robin
leaned over to Nikki. "How long has it
been?" she whispered.

Nikki looked at her watch. "Thirteen minutes," she said.

Robin slumped back in her chair.

More time passed. Pages rustled as magazines were read. Someone coughed. One of
the receptionists left on her lunch break.

Finally the door opened. It was
Annamarie. "Robin, you can come back in,"
she said with a smile.

Nikki squeezed her hand. Lacey gave her a

serious nod. Robin tried to smile at them, but she failed. She turned and walked toward the doctor.

It was funny, Robin thought suddenly, how in the time it took to go from one moment to the next, her whole life could change. As she passed through the door, Robin realized that she'd had her first inkling of what being an adult must be like. You couldn't stick your head in the sand, Robin thought as she followed Annamarie's white-jacketed back down the hall. You had to deal with things, no matter what.

She walked into the office and sat in the chair by the desk. Annamarie opened a file with her name on it. Robin gripped the arms of her chair. Whatever the news, she was finally ready to hear it.

"Lunchtime," Mrs. Tate called cheerfully, poking her head into the back room. "Brittany, why don't you go to the deli and get sandwiches for all of us?"

That would never do. Brittany thought fast. "I've got a better idea, Mom. You're going to be working hard all day long. Why don't you go out for a bit? Then when you come back, Ruby can go. You both need a break."

Mrs. Tate looked thoughtful. "You know,

that might be better. Thank you, Brittany."
She took off her apron. "I'll be back in half
an hour."

Brittany and Ruby worked in silence for a
while. Then, as Ruby bent over to retrieve a
fallen iris, she suddenly sighed heavily.

"Are you okay?" Brittany asked.

Ruby smiled. "Oh, I'm fine. Just man
trouble. I had a fight with my boyfriend last
night."

Brittany nodded sympathetically. "Anything I can do?"

"No, Brittany, but thanks. You know how
it is—you don't feel better until you can
make up."

"I know. I'm sure you will," Brittany said
soothingly, but her mind was racing. Ruby
had been awfully quiet. Could this "man
trouble" of Ruby's help her plan?

Mrs. Tate returned from lunch in twenty
minutes. Ruby grabbed her purse, straightened an iris, and left. By now, her pretty face
was flushed and upset looking.

Mrs. Tate watched her go with a frown on
her face, but she didn't say a word to Brittany. She immediately put her apron back on
and went back to work.

Brittany took her time. She measured
green satin ribbon and began cutting off the
strips Ruby had wanted.

"Everything looks so beautiful," Mrs. Tate said, leaning over to smell a gardenia. "Ruby's done a terrific job."

Brittany sighed.

"I don't know what I'd do without her," Mrs. Tate went on.

Brittany sighed again.

Her mother looked up, concerned. "Is something wrong, sweetheart?"

Brittany put down her scissors. "Oh, Mom. I shouldn't say anything at all."

"What, dear?"

Brittany leaned against the worktable. "It's just that, well, I think you should know. Ruby may be unhappy here."

"What?" Mrs. Tate looked shocked. "That's impossible."

Brittany shrugged and picked up her scissors again. "I could be wrong," she said, her voice uncertain.

After a minute Mrs. Tate said faintly, "She *did* seem quiet today. Did she talk to you about this?"

"It's not that she doesn't like working for you," Brittany said. She didn't want her mother to freak out completely. "She loves the shop."

"Then what is it?" Mrs. Tate peered at her. "This is terrible. I can't imagine Ruby not coming to me." With quick, jerky motions, Mrs. Tate began to tie up bunches of lily of the valley with the ribbons Brittany had cut. "What is it, Brittany? Is it her salary?"

Brittany felt uncomfortable under her mother's penetrating gaze. "No, no. That's not it at all."

"Then what?" Her mother sat down weakly on the bench. "I can't lose Ruby."

"It's not a question of money," Brittany said delicately. She sat down next to her mother. "I think it's just that she's been working here for a year, and she feels you don't trust her."

"Don't trust her? What did she say?"

"It's not anything she said, exactly, but—"

"Of course I trust her!" Mrs. Tate interrupted wildly. "She's a genius! Brittany, this just doesn't sound like Ruby."

"That's exactly what I thought." Brittany shrugged. "Mom, you know how you have to do everything yourself. Another flower shop might give someone like Ruby more responsibility. I could be wrong about this, but maybe if you let her handle something herself . . ." Brittany paused. "You can't ever tell her I mentioned this. She'd die."

"Of course I won't mention it," Mrs. Tate said distractedly. "Oh, why did this have to happen today?"

Brittany said nothing. She waited a beat. Then another.

Mrs. Tate's chin lifted. "Then again," she said slowly, "this might be the perfect time."

Brittany conquered the look of triumph that almost flashed in her eyes. "Why, Mom?"

"I'll let her handle the country club dance by herself!" Mrs. Tate exclaimed. "That would show her how much I value her judgment. What do you think, Brittany?"

Brittany pretended to ponder this. "Oh, Mom. Do you really think you should?"

Mrs. Tate frowned. "Maybe you're right. It's a big job."

"But on the other hand, Ruby could definitely handle it," Brittany said quickly.

Mrs. Tate hesitated for a long, agonizing moment. Then she nodded decisively and threw her arms around Brittany. "Thank you, honey. You saved the day."

She sure had. "Oh, don't mention it, Mom. I was glad to help," Brittany said modestly.

12

"Well, I won't torture you, Robin," the doctor said. "You're not pregnant."

The relief was like a sudden plunge into a cold, clear pool. "I'm not? Are you sure?" Robin said.

Annamarie nodded. "I'm sure."

Robin jumped up from her chair. "I can't believe it! This is great. Oh, thank you so much."

"I don't think," Annamarie said dryly, "that I had anything to do with it."

Robin sank back down into her chair. "Thank you anyway," she said. Then she remembered Nikki and Lacey. "Can I go tell my friends?" she asked.

"Not so fast," Annamarie said. "We have to talk about some things. First of all, I need to ask you some questions. Do you have a steady boyfriend, Robin?"

She nodded. "His name is Calvin," she said faintly. It was one thing to put off Nikki and Lacey about the details, but Robin had a feeling Annamarie wouldn't be stopped.

"Have you and Calvin had sexual relations?" Annamarie asked gently.

Robin blushed and looked down at the floor. "No. I mean, we haven't made love, not even once. But we came really close and — I guess I just jumped to conclusions."

Annamarie nodded. "I see. What's important here, Robin, is for you to feel you have control over what you do with your boyfriend. Because you do. It's a decision that you can make yourself. And I hope you can talk about it with him."

"That might be kind of embarrassing," Robin mumbled.

"You seem a little embarrassed now, too. Are you?" The doctor's gaze was steady.

Robin nodded. Embarrassed? She'd be delighted if she could sink through the floor.

"Well, if you're too embarrassed to talk about this with me or Cal, perhaps you should think about whether you're ready to do it at all."

Robin didn't answer. Her face was hot. She was sure her cheeks were a lovely shade of magenta by now.

"Do you love each other?" Annamarie asked gently.

Robin nodded.

"Well, then I think you two can talk together. It might be a little difficult at first. But you might find that he wants to discuss it, too. The two of you can decide how intimate you want to be. But be sure it's what *you* want." Annamarie leaned closer. "The point is, Robin, that you almost had to make an adult woman's decision. Whether or not to have, or keep, a child. Do you feel ready for that?"

Robin shook her head. "No. I just felt scared and alone."

"Then you may not be ready for full intimacy in your relationship with Cal. But you can still be close. Robin, will you do something for me?"

"Anything," Robin said fervently.

Annamarie laughed. "I want you to come back and see me if you decide to go further. You need to be well-informed, but I'd do a lot of thinking first and a lot of exploring of your own feelings. Remember that it's an adult decision, and it has adult consequences. Okay?"

"Okay," Robin agreed. She'd already made her decision. But it might not matter, she realized. Now that the relief had worn off, she remembered that she and Calvin weren't even speaking.

"Now we return to the problem you came in here for," Annamarie said. "Your missed period. Has your life changed in any way in the past couple of months? Your diet, or exercise?"

"Well, I've been training pretty hard," Robin admitted. "I'm on the swim team. Maybe I've been overdoing it a little, especially since I was so nervous. And then, with falling in love with Cal and all, I guess I wasn't eating too well. Is that what you mean?"

Annamarie nodded. "That's exactly what I mean. Sometimes poor diet, strenuous exercise, and stress can interrupt a woman's cycle. But just to make sure, I want you to make an appointment with your regular doctor and get a full checkup. You don't have to say you were afraid you were pregnant if you don't want to. But do tell him you've missed your period. All right?"

"All right," Robin said. "I guess I'm due for a checkup anyway."

"Good." Annamarie smiled. "Now, why don't you go on out there and tell those worried-looking friends of yours the good news."

With another thank-you and a hasty good-bye, Robin left the office and dashed down the hall. She burst into the outer room. One look at her smiling face and Nikki and Lacey jumped up. The three of them met in the middle of the room and hugged.

"I told you so," Lacey said with brimming eyes.

When the girls pulled apart, they realized that they were the center of attention. Sheepishly, they gathered their hats and sunglasses and filed out of the waiting room.

The sun was shining, and the cool air felt delicious as they stepped onto the sidewalk. The girls stopped and looked at one another. Then, without a word, they all threw their hats in the air as high as they could. They laughed and cheered as the hats fell to the pavement.

Picking their hats up, the three of them ran to the car, still laughing with relief.

Robin grew sober as Nikki unlocked the door. "I don't know how I would have gotten through all this without you two," she said. "You're the best."

Nikki and Lacey smiled at her. "That's

because we care about you, Fisher," Nikki said.

Robin collapsed in the front seat. "I don't deserve this, but I don't care! This is the best day of my life!"

"Does that include this morning?" Nikki teased.

Robin shuddered. "And how about tonight?" she said. "What's going to happen at the dance? Cal could refuse to talk to me. What will I say to him?"

"You'll think of something. Anyway, once he sees you in that dress, he'll listen to anything you say," Nikki said. She turned to Lacey. "You should see this dress."

"It's stretchy purple lace, but underneath it has silk material that's an incredible shade of electric green," Robin said enthusiastically. "I mean, it sounds weird, but it is *so* hot. The weirdest thing about it was that Nikki, Miss Classic Style, picked it out."

"I knew something flashy would cheer you up," Nikki said, smiling.

"I wish you could come, Lacey," Robin said.

"Me, too," Nikki agreed. "It would be much more fun."

"I wish I could be there," Lacey said faintly. She sank against the back seat and looked out the window, feeling a bit left out.

If only she didn't have to work tonight, but she couldn't have afforded a new dress, anyway. Her mind returned to the topic she'd been thinking about all week, when she wasn't worrying about Robin. Money.

Nikki glanced at Lacey in the rearview mirror and frowned. "Are you okay back there?" she asked.

Lacey bounced up and rested her elbows on the front seat. "I'm okay. As a matter of fact, I might be great. I've got an idea I want to try out on you two." She grinned. "It's a get-rich-quick scheme, and I think it might just work!"

The country club was glittering with tiny white lights as Brittany and Jack drove up. A valet emerged from the shadows of the porch and opened Brittany's car door. She slipped out, feeling like a queen. Jack came around the car and gave her his arm.

"Did I tell you that you look beautiful tonight?" he asked, standing back a bit to look at her.

"I think I heard you mention it once or twice," Brittany said with a gracious smile. The effect of the dress on Jack was everything she'd hoped.

Jack checked their coats, then led Brittany through the lobby toward the elegant back room where the dance would be held. She almost gasped when they reached it. The place looked so romantic and beautiful.

There were thin gold tapers on each table, and masses of waxy white gardenias floating in huge crystal bowls on side tables. The room looked simple and elegant, but Brittany knew how much effort it had cost. She saw Ruby off in a corner, arranging a tiny bouquet of lilies of the valley. Intent on her task, she didn't notice Brittany. Fortunately.

"Amazing flowers," Jack said in her ear. "I usually don't notice things like that. Usually they just have some bouquets thrown around."

It was on the tip of Brittany's tongue to tell Jack that her mother's shop had done the arrangements. For the first time she didn't feel embarrassed to admit it.

"And in that white dress, you match everything so perfectly," Jack said. "Amazing!"

The moment had passed. Brittany couldn't explain how she'd been able to plan this particular effect.

Brittany let Jack sweep her into a dance. Soon the music and the strength of his arms drove every other thought out of her head. When she saw Ruby slipping into her coat and leaving, she knew her troubles were over.

Now she could relax and check out who was looking her over. Most of the girls were staring at her dress with obvious envy. She saw Nikki and Tim dance by, Nikki in a black dress with tiny pink rose buds. Very sweet, Brittany thought. It was hard to believe that Nikki could be pregnant. Nobody in that kind of trouble could look so nauseatingly happy.

The song ended, another began, and one of Jack's college friends asked Brittany to dance. Jack glowered as she went off with him and Brittany felt a thrill shoot through her.

Throughout the evening Brittany never lacked for partners, and she was happy to see that Jack appeared to be a little jealous of her popularity. Finally, as she finished still another dance, she looked around for her date.

"Brittany, may I have this dance?"

It was Jeremy Pratt. Annoyed, Brittany glanced around again for Jack.

"Come on, Brittany. Let's show these people how it's done." Jeremy took her hand and gave it a none-too-gentle tug. Throwing him an irritated look, Brittany sighed and followed him.

"I like your dress," Jeremy murmured as he held her a little too close.

She pushed against him slightly, gaining a

millimeter of distance between them.
Jeremy could be such a pain. "Thanks."

"So you're going out with Jack Reilly
these days," he said casually.

"Mmmm," Brittany replied, looking over
her shoulder at the crowd. She noticed Robin
Fisher walk into the room. The Moose was
wearing an incredible deep purple dress,
very short. Brittany had to admit she looked
fabulous—and happy. She couldn't possibly
be the one who was pregnant, either. Now,
where was Lacey Dupree?

Jeremy broke into her thoughts. "I was
pretty surprised to see you here. Until I saw
you were with Jack, I mean."

Brittany looked up at him. What was
Jeremy getting at?

"I know your parents aren't members," Jeremy went on in his smooth voice.
"Usually these things are for members
only."

"Don't be silly, Jeremy," Brittany responded, frowning. "Members can bring
guests."

"You know, I've talked about that with my
dad," Jeremy said. "Sure, members can
bring guests. The problem is when guests use
the privilege to pretend they're actually
members. Can you imagine anyone doing
that, Brittany? I was thinking of asking Jack

Reilly about it. Do you think he'd be interested?"

It was amazing that such a low, cultivated voice could come from such a reptile. Brittany felt her cheeks burn. Jeremy was going to drop that piece of information in Jack's lap.

Then why was he telling her first? Just to make her squirm?

She might as well get it over with. "Do you want something from me, Jeremy?" Brittany asked. This time, she didn't try to disguise the contempt in her voice.

Jeremy wheeled her around and drew her closer, his mouth close to her ear. Brittany shuddered.

"Kim looks fabulous tonight, don't you think? That dark blue dress—mmmm. I'd like to ask her out, but I know she's very fussy. Do you think she'd go out with me?"

"How should I know?" Brittany asked crossly.

"I'm just asking because I know Kim's your best friend. I'd hate to ask her and be turned down, you know what I mean? Maybe you could see that I'm not. If I'm busy with Kim, I might not have time to talk to Jack."

Brittany was caught. How could she throw her best friend into the clutches of Jeremy Pratt? He was lower than a snake's belly. But was he *so* low that he would tell Jack that the Tates weren't members of the club? May-be Jack wouldn't care, but he probably wouldn't like the fact that she'd lied to him.

Then again, Kim hadn't been very nice to her lately. And maybe Kim wouldn't mind dating Jeremy Pratt. The girl couldn't stand him, of course, but there was nothing like a little bit of interest on a guy's part for a quick change of heart. Jeremy *was* good-looking, and Kim was just as big a snob as he was. They had that in common, at least.

Brittany sighed. It didn't matter how Kim had been acting lately; she and Kim had always had their ups and downs. She was still her best friend. Brittany hated the thought of having to talk her into this.

But she couldn't lose Jack. And, she real-ized, looking at Jeremy's smug smile, he knew it.

"All right, Jeremy," Brittany said as the music ended. "You win. I'll talk to Kim for you."

"That's great," he said. "Right now?"

"Sure," Brittany agreed, but she couldn't resist a small retaliation. As she turned, she stepped on his Italian loafer with the heel of her gold pump. Jeremy howled.

"Oh, how clumsy of me," Brittany said, wide-eyed. "Are you okay?"

"No. I'm not." Now it was Jeremy's turn to be furious.

"I'm so sorry, Jeremy," Brittany cooed. "I had no idea that snakes had feet."

Robin was nervous, but she was also determined. How could she let her own boyfriend intimidate her? Even if she *was* in love with him.

When she saw Calvin, though, she almost turned around and went home again. Did he have to look so great? She could see other girls eyeing him, but he wasn't dancing. As a matter of fact, he looked pretty miserable.

That pushed Robin forward. As she approached, Calvin spotted her and swallowed. Then he looked away.

Robin came up beside him. "Hi."

Calvin stared out at the dancers. "Hi."

"I want to talk to you," Robin said.

Calvin shrugged. "I don't think we have anything to talk about, do you?"

"Yes, we do," Robin insisted. "I wanted to tell you why I've been acting so weird lately."

Calvin turned and gave her a long look. "You know what? I don't care anymore."

Robin felt like crying. Here she was, all dressed up, ready to spill everything to Calvin, and he wouldn't listen.

What had she been doing to him lately? Robin asked herself bitterly. Avoiding him, pretending everything was fine, then pretending she didn't care. What did she expect? He was treating her exactly the way she'd treated him.

But, Robin thought with a small gleam of hope, hadn't she really cared underneath? No matter what she'd said, what she'd done.

If Calvin still loved her, she could reach him.

Resolutely, Robin took Calvin by the arm. Before he could open his mouth, she rushed in.

"You're coming with me. Don't say no, don't say you can't, don't say you don't want to, don't say you don't have to. Because you do."

13

They stared at each other for a long moment. Finally Calvin nodded. "All right," he said.

Neither of them spoke as they headed swiftly through the crowd toward the French doors at the end of the room. The night air was chilly as they stepped outside, and Robin crossed her arms.

Cal spun around when they reached the pool. "So, talk."

"I don't know how to say this," Robin began, "so I'm just going to say it. I thought I was pregnant. I found out today that I'm not."

Cal looked at her, dumbfounded. "What?"

"I didn't want to tell you," Robin said. "I thought I could keep all the worry inside. But I just got more and more scared."

"But we never—"

"I know," Robin told him. "But we almost did. And I had some of the signs, so—" She shrugged. "I started thinking it was possible. You know how I love to exaggerate. I guess I went too far this time," she said feebly.

Calvin didn't smile. He thrust his hands into his pockets, confusion and anger still on his face. "Why didn't you tell me, Robin?"

"Because I didn't know for sure," Robin answered. "It didn't seem fair to have you upset if it turned out to be a false alarm. You were busy, and— Oh, things just kept happening. Everyone at school thought I was pregnant. Or that Nikki or Lacey was. Didn't you hear the rumors?"

"Nobody tells me anything," Calvin said glumly.

Robin looked down at the ground. "Oh, Cal. It wasn't that I didn't trust you. I just knew how worried you'd be. And your grades are so important."

Calvin frowned. "Robin, please don't say that. It makes me sound terrible. I know I study hard, but do you really think all that stuff is as important as you are to me?"

"I guess not," she whispered. "Is it still true?"

Cal took off his jacket and draped it tenderly around Robin's shoulders. Then he cupped her face in his hands and looked into her eyes. "I love you," he said. "And if you *ever* keep anything like this from me again," he added, "I'll kill you."

Robin smiled. "I promise I won't. Oh, Cal, please forgive me."

She leaned against him, and Cal hugged her fiercely. They kissed—a long, warm kiss. Robin knew he wasn't mad anymore.

Finally Robin pulled away. "There are a few other things I have to say," she said.

"Uh-oh," Cal said with a grin.

Robin grinned, too, but then she grew serious. "I don't want this to happen ever again," she said. "I realized something in the last week, Cal. I love you, but I'm not ready for, well, for this kind of responsibility. I want to take everything slower. We can't just be swept away. We have to decide that we're not ready. Well, actually, I decided that already." She let out a breath. "Is that okay?"

"Of course it's okay," Calvin said.

"The thing is, Cal," Robin said softly, "I miss my friends. We've been spending so much time together—"

Cal took in a breath. Had she hurt him again? "You want us to see each other less?" he said.

Robin shook her head. "No way. But maybe we could double-date more. With Nikki and Tim or Lacey and Rick. And hang around Leon's or the Loft with them more than we do. We don't always have to be alone." She hesitated. "Would that be okay?"

Calvin grinned. "It sounds great. Maybe I did take you away from everyone." He kissed her lightly on the forehead. "I think you're right. We should take things slower."

"Oh, Cal." Robin kissed him softly.

"I think we'd better go inside," Calvin said. "You're shivering. I don't want you to come down with a cold now that we've made up. Besides," he added, pulling away and looking at her in the moonlight, "I want to see that dress. And I want everyone else to see that I have the most beautiful girlfriend in the world."

"And the most difficult," Robin said impishly.

Calvin laughed. "Well, at least she's never dull," he said.

Brittany hunted down Kim in the ladies' room. She was leaning forward in the mirror, checking out her makeup.

"You look fabulous tonight," Brittany said as she took out some blusher from her purse. "That's a killer dress."

"Thanks," Kim said. "You look great, too. Jack can't keep his eyes off you."

Brittany carefully applied the blusher high on her cheekbones. "I really like him," she said.

Kim brushed her smooth blond hair. "Eric's okay, but kind of dull. All that school spirit can get tiresome. I mean, rah rah — blah. And his car! He borrowed his father's. It smells like cigars." Kim grimaced. "I'm glad you're having fun, but it's too bad the dance isn't as exciting for the rest of us."

Brittany saw her opening. "It could be, you know," she said mysteriously.

Kim looked at her in the mirror with raised eyebrows. "What does that mean?"

"It means that Jeremy Pratt only needs a little encouragement to flip over you completely."

Kim made a sour face. "You've got to be kidding. Jeremy?"

"I'd think about it," Brittany said casually. "He's very cute *and* very available."

"Jeremy?" Kim looked confused. "Brittany, you know he's a stuck-up jerk."

"I know he *seems* that way sometimes," Brittany said. "But let's face it, Kim — he's got style — and a Porsche. He's a Pratt, after all. And he thinks you're gorgeous."

"He said that?" Kim asked in disbelief.

"He did." Brittany nodded. Kim was

studying herself in the mirror again, a small smile curving her lips. Brittany had hit the right buttons, all right. "You should have heard him going on and on about your dress, and what a knockout you were," Brittany continued. "He said you put every girl here to shame. It wasn't very polite." Brittany sniffed. "I was dancing with him at the time."

"Jeremy Pratt." Kim seemed to try the name on for size while she dreamily continued to regard her reflection.

It was time for the final push. "I don't know, though," Brittany went on. "I can't imagine the two of you together. Jeremy and Kim—everybody would *die*. You'd practically run the school."

Kim's expression brightened. "He is pretty cute," she said grudgingly.

"Oh, definitely," Brittany agreed.

"And he does have style." Kim looked thoughtful. "And he *is* a Pratt."

"They practically run the River Heights social scene," Brittany added.

"Maybe I will go out with him," Kim said. "Once."

"I think you should give it a shot," Brittany said with a shrug. "Why not?"

"Why not?" Kim said with a laugh. She linked her arm through Brittany's. "Thanks, pal."

"You're welcome." They walked out arm in arm, laughing together. Jeremy caught Brittany's eye, and she nodded. He started toward Kim confidently. Mission accomplished. Brittany heaved a sigh of relief.

There was a touch on her elbow. Brittany turned to find Jack by her side.

"I've missed you," he said, smiling. "Do you think you could dance with your date for a change?"

"I think that could be arranged," Brittany said lightly.

The band was playing a slow, romantic number. Brittany leaned her cheek against Jack's shoulder. They swayed to the tune, and Jack held her very close.

"You know," he whispered in her ear, "I could get used to this."

"Good," Brittany whispered back. She pressed closer to him.

They circled around slowly to the music. As they turned, Brittany gazed out the dark windows of the club. It took several long seconds for her to recognize the tiny face pressed up against the window, watching intently. *Tamara!* Behind her, another beady-eyed face loomed.

"I don't believe it," she said.

"What?"

Brittany pointed in horror. Jack laughed.

"I think I might be flattered," he said. "Come on, let's go."

Grimly, Brittany followed Jack outside. They hunted for a few minutes, then found Tamara and her friend, Debbie, scrunched up behind a net at the tennis courts. Brittany was furious. Her sister was going to spoil the whole evening! How dare she pull this trick!

"I thought I warned you to leave us alone!" Brittany hissed. "How did you get here?"

Tamara looked at the ground. "I told Mom and Dad I was going over to Debbie's house next door. Then we took a bus and walked the rest of the way here. I just wanted to show Jack to Debbie, that's all."

Jack winked at Brittany. "I didn't realize I was such a big attraction," he said.

Brittany was furious. "Mom and Dad will kill you," she said, grabbing Tamara by the collar like a stray dog. "And I'd like to, myself. You shouldn't be out at night alone. Debbie, you should be ashamed of yourself, too."

"Sorry," Debbie said, hanging her head.

"We were perfectly safe," Tamara insisted.

Brittany sighed. "What am I going to do with you two now? I'll have to call Dad and ask him to pick you both up."

"I have a better idea," Jack broke in. "Let's take them home ourselves."

"What?" Brittany looked at him, astonished. The dance wasn't anywhere near over. Was he having a terrible time? Tamara was going to get it, that was for sure.

"I'd rather be alone with you, anyway," Jack said in a low voice. He looked at her meaningfully. "All alone."

Brittany felt an odd feeling in the pit of her stomach. Her heart raced. Jack had been so much more romantic lately. But long kisses on her front porch didn't seem to be what Jack had in mind this time. "All right," she agreed, "but let me talk to Tamara first."

"I'll get your coat," Jack said. He took off and went back inside the club.

Brittany glared at Tamara, her hands on her hips. It was clear she'd have to take a different approach. "Okay," she said finally. "Here's the deal. You butt out of my life, and I'll teach you some things."

"Like what?" Tamara asked warily.

"Like how not to hang around a guy like a puppy to get him to notice you. And how to talk to him once he *does* notice you. A guy your own age," Brittany added. "Is it a deal?"

Tamara hesitated. She looked at Debbie, who nodded furiously. Finally Tamara said, "Okay. Deal."

"Good." Brittany spun around, dragging

the two girls with her. Despite the queasy feeling in her stomach, she couldn't wait to be alone with Jack.

With Tamara and Debbie safely dropped off with a stern Mr. and Mrs. Tate, Jack drove to Moon Lake. Brittany felt her heart flutter as they pulled into a beautiful spot she'd never seen before. Pine trees towered over the car, and a full moon illuminated a silver path on the dark water.

"I thought I knew every inch of this lake," Brittany said softly. "I've never been here before, though."

"It's my favorite spot," Jack said, looking out at the lake. "I discovered it when I was camping a few years ago. They put a road in last summer, so I guess more people will be coming here now."

"That's too bad," Brittany said as Jack put his arm around her. "I mean, I guess you'd want to keep it private," she said.

"Yes, I would. Very private." Jack's head descended, and his lips came down on hers hard.

Brittany kissed him back, but her mind was working furiously. The truth was that she was a little bit scared.

It was obvious that Jack wasn't nervous in the least. He kissed her as though he knew she couldn't possibly refuse him. That scared and thrilled Brittany at the same time.

When she kissed a guy from River Heights High, there was never any real temptation. But Jack Reilly was definitely temptation. Brittany felt herself move closer and slip her arms around him. Wasn't that what he expected? For the first time, Brittany began to see the scary side of dating a college man.

Jack kissed her neck. It was clear he was heading somewhere that Brittany didn't think she should go.

An image floated into her mind of a frightened-looking Robin and Nikki at the drugstore. Suddenly she knew what that fear meant. She didn't want to end up like that unfortunate girl, whoever she was.

She also thought of how hard she'd schemed and manipulated to keep Jack's interest. Lying to her mother, setting Kim up with Jeremy Pratt. How much was dating Jack Reilly really worth?

Jack sighed. "This gearshift is killing me. Why don't we get comfortable in the back seat?" He touched her chin. "You're so beautiful in this moonlight, Brittany."

What should she do? What did college girls do? Brittany wondered frantically. Was Jack used to a girl who responded to him without regrets, who wasn't afraid of her pounding heart and perspiring hands?

Jack trailed his lips slowly down to her neck again. Brittany's heart fluttered wildly in her chest. She'd worked so hard to get him. She wouldn't, couldn't lose him. But just how far should she go to keep him?

———————————

Brittany's romance with Jack has really heated up. Will a love triangle cool him off? Lacey is saving for a car. Can her favorite rock group help her get the money she needs? Find out in River Heights #4, _Stolen Kisses_.